"Tess, have you changed your mind about…us?"

"Maybe…I don't know. I've never felt like this, and when I'm with you, I can't seem to think straight."

"I'll take that as a compliment," Jack said, his gaze straying to the swell of creamy flesh visible above the robe she clutched to her bosom.

Her eyes narrowed. She knew him well enough to know what he was thinking.

"Jack." Her tone was a warning. "There are people in the next room. People who would have to be stupid not to know what we were doing before they arrived."

He swallowed hard and nodded, then turned to go. Before pulling the door shut behind him, he whispered, "Next time, I vote we don't answer the door when someone rings the bell."

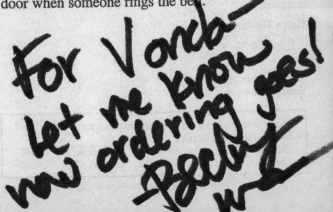

Dear Reader,

As Silhouette's yearlong anniversary celebration continues, Romance again delivers six unique stories about the poignant journey from courtship to commitment.

Teresa Southwick invites you back to STORKVILLE, USA, where a wealthy playboy has the gossips stumped with his latest transaction: *The Acquired Bride*...and her triplet kids! *New York Times* bestselling author Kasey Michaels contributes the second title in THE CHANDLERS REQUEST... miniseries, *Jessie's Expecting*. Judy Christenberry spins off her popular THE CIRCLE K SISTERS with a story involving a blizzard, a roadside motel with one bed left, a gorgeous, honor-bound rancher...and his *Snowbound Sweetheart*.

New from Donna Clayton is SINGLE DOCTOR DADS! In the premiere story of this wonderful series, a first-time father strikes *The Nanny Proposal* with a woman whose timely hiring quickly proves less serendipitous and more carefully, *lovingly*, staged.... Lilian Darcy pens yet another edgy, uplifting story with *Raising Baby Jane*. And debut author Jackie Braun delivers pure romantic fantasy as a down-on-her-luck waitress receives an intriguing order from the man of her dreams: *One Fiancée To Go, Please*.

Next month, look for the exciting finales of STORKVILLE, USA and THE CHANDLERS REQUEST... And the wait is over as Carolyn Zane's BRUBAKER BRIDES make their grand reappearance!

Happy Reading!

Mary Theresa Hussey

Mary Theresa Hussey
Senior Editor

Please address questions and book requests to:
Silhouette Reader Service
U.S.: 3010 Walden Ave., P.O. Box 1325, Buffalo, NY 14269
Canadian: P.O. Box 609, Fort Erie, Ont. L2A 5X3

One Fiancée To Go, Please

JACKIE BRAUN

SILHOUETTE *Romance*

Published by Silhouette Books

America's Publisher of Contemporary Romance

For my sister, Donna Warrick,
who believed in me even when I had doubts.

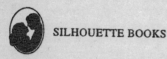

SILHOUETTE BOOKS

ISBN 0-373-19479-X

ONE FIANCÉE TO GO, PLEASE

Visit Silhouette at www.eHarlequin.com

Printed in U.S.A.

JACKIE BRAUN

wrote her first book, a murder mystery, in elementary school. To get some of the heart-pounding scenes just right, she first acted them out in her family's suburban Detroit backyard. The neighbors are probably still talking about the skinny blond kid who had all the imaginary friends. The handwritten pages of that masterpiece are in her basement somewhere. They may be misplaced, but she never put aside her desire to write. She earned her bachelor's degree from Central Michigan University and has spent the past thirteen years working as a journalist, mostly penning editorials at a mid-Michigan newspaper. Weaving tales of fiction, however, has remained her first love. She lives with her husband in Flushing, Michigan.

Dear Reader,

Christmas arrived a little early for me last year. Four days before Santa shimmied down the chimney with his sack of presents, Silhouette Books called bearing the ultimate gift for a writer: a book contract.

For me, this isn't just *any* book. It's the first one I've sold after many years of hard work and high hopes, so I am especially excited to share it with you.

Someone recently asked me where I got the idea for this story. Writers find stories everywhere, even in everyday situations. As it happens, this one nearly landed on me while I waited for a cab to the airport. I was sipping orange juice in a hotel lobby when I bobbled the cup and narrowly avoided spilling it down my shirt. Inspiration struck, however, and I wrote the opening scene in a spiral notebook on my flight home. Let's just say that seat in coach felt especially cramped with Jack, Tess and me all sitting in it.

For several weeks after that, I booted up my computer almost daily to "visit" with Jack and Tess. As they struggled with their growing attraction, sometimes they surprised even me with the way their story unfolded.

Writers say finishing a book is a great thrill, and it is. It offers a sense of accomplishment that's difficult to describe. But I was almost sad to finish the final scene. I didn't want it to end, because I enjoyed spending time with Jack and Tess.

I hope you will, too.

Sincerely,

Jackie Braun

Chapter One

"**O**rder up!" Earl Lester barked.

Tess Donovan stood at the counter just outside the diner's small kitchen making a fresh pot of coffee. She jumped at the gruffly issued command, sending grounds flying. Exhaling slowly, she smoothed a stray wisp of hair back from her cheek and turned to the order window. Earl stood on the opposite side, a toothy grin spreading over his leathery face.

"A little edgy today, Red?" he inquired, all innocence.

"You know the saying—too much caffeine and not enough sleep make Tess an edgy girl. Midterms," she reminded him needlessly. For six years she had worked full-time for Earl while freelancing for the local newspaper on weekends in the fall and working her way toward a journalism degree in the evenings. She figured he knew her schedule about as well as she did.

"So does exhaustion," he reminded her with a

pointed look. He motioned with his chin to the steaming crock. "It's getting cold, Red."

"This stuff has too much chili powder in it ever to be anything but blazing hot," she replied, sending him a saucy wink as she loaded the bowl onto her tray. Then she hurried away, the tray held high over her head, her pockets heavy with tip money.

Wednesdays at Earl's Place generally left Tess with enough time between taking food orders and clearing tables to study for her classes. But Earl had advertised a dinner special in the newspaper this week, and it seemed half the population of Pleasant River, Michigan, had turned out to take advantage of the deal. It was just Tess's luck that one waitress had called in sick and another had had car trouble and would be late. Tess had agreed to fill in after her shift ended, at least until her political science class at seven. She had planned to use the in-between time to catch up on the seemingly endless barrage of reading assignments, but, with the holidays just around the corner, the extra tip money was too tempting to pass up.

"Hon, I need more coffee," the burly trucker at table ten called as she passed. She managed to sidestep him in time to avoid the fanny pat he had bestowed on her twice already.

Three tables ahead sat the man who had ordered the chili. He was impeccably dressed in a navy wool suit, crisp white shirt and muted print tie, all of which screamed expensive. He looked as if he could be a banker or a lawyer or some other white-collar professional, not the usual sort to come into Earl's greasy little joint. He sat alone with a *Wall Street Journal* spread out on the table in front of him, open to the stock page. But he wasn't reading it. He was watching her. And the level, measuring look he gave Tess made her pulse pick up speed.

Handsome didn't begin to do him justice. He had a strong jaw, wide-spaced eyes the color of jade, and a nose that listed slightly to the left and gave the impression he had once played contact sports. He wore his tawny hair short, but Tess had a hunch that if it were allowed to grow long it would have a tendency to curl, much like her own.

The crowded diner seemed to fade into the background as their gazes held. The pounding of her heart drowned out the din of patrons as she was drawn forward on legs that felt too rubbery to hold her weight. Ridiculous, she told herself, bemused by this uncharacteristic reaction to a man, but she couldn't manage to break eye contact or to reel in her giddy pulse.

At least not until the tyke at table four scooted off his mother's lap and toddled directly into Tess's path. It seemed a minor miracle that she managed to side-step the boy at all; too many hours on her feet had dulled her reflexes, and the man claimed nearly all of her attention. But she didn't have time to ponder the near collision or to congratulate herself for avoiding it. In the instant it took to dodge the little boy, the steaming crock of chili lost its purchase on her tilted tray. Helpless, she watched it slide off, striking the gorgeous businessman just above the breastbone with a dull thud that sent its contents spewing. Kidney beans, onions and bits of ground beef oozed down the man's broad chest like a mini-mudslide.

"What the...!" he broke off an oath, instinctively pushing away Tess, who very nearly found herself in his lap along with the remains of his dinner. She grabbed the edge of the table to upright herself, then stood back in mortification and surveyed the damage.

"Oh, no!" The hand she clamped over her mouth barely muffled her cry. Unless the dry cleaners could perform miracles, the man's very nice and very expensive-looking suit was also very ruined. What, she wondered, would a suit like that cost? She had the awful feeling she was about to find out. The tip money weighing down her pockets suddenly felt inconsequential.

Tess peered anxiously over her shoulder, hoping Earl had not witnessed her latest debacle. In the past week alone she had given the wrong change to three customers, botched a number of meal orders, and sent an entire tray of brown coffee mugs crashing to the tiled floor. She didn't think she could bear another lecture on how she should get more sleep or cut back on her class load. Her luck seemed to be holding. While she had captured the attention of nearly every diner in the place, the swinging doors to the kitchen remained blessedly still. She turned back to the man and gaped in horrified silence as he eased himself out of the booth with as much dignity as the situation would allow. Globs of chili dropped to the floor in a sickening chorus of plops as he straightened.

He grimaced, attempting to hold the soiled shirt front away from his skin by pinching it between his thumb and index finger. A gold cufflink winked at his wrist, catching Tess's attention. French cuffs, she thought with an inward sigh, and another imaginary dollar sign appeared before her eyes.

"I'm *so* sorry, sir," she said in a shaky whisper. Snatching some napkins from the table dispenser, she began blotting his soggy tie and wiping the stubborn bits of ground beef from his shirt. She hesitated when she reached the shiny buckle of his leather belt. His lap was covered with chili as well, but she dared go no farther south with the mass of matted napkins. He grasped her wrist lightly, as if he thought she might have the audacity to continue downward, and she felt a blush creep from her chin to her cheeks. She couldn't quite meet his eyes.

"You've done enough, thanks," he bit out between gritted teeth, releasing her hand and grabbing the napkins from her. He swiped at the stain that had bloomed a rusty red on his shirt and turned his navy suit a dingy shade of brown. The mirthless little laugh he issued made Tess feel even worse.

"I'll get you some more chili if you'd like. Or anything else from the menu," she offered, eager to make amends.

"I'll take my check."

"I am truly sorry," she repeated. Any minute now, she thought, he would be mentioning the cost of his suit and demanding compensation. "I'm not usually so clumsy. I just didn't see the little boy until it was too late."

He nodded grimly. "My check."

"Oh, no charge," Tess assured him, offering a tentative smile in the hope of coaxing one out in return. "Really, I insist. Dinner's on me."

Her words drew out more than a smile. Humor, unexpected but definitely welcome, danced in the man's green eyes a moment before she heard the first deep rumble of his laughter.

"Dinner's on somebody, lady, but I don't think it's you." To Tess's immense relief, his irritation seemed to evaporate. He flashed a grin that showed off straight white teeth, and a dimple tugged in his left cheek. Charmed, Tess smiled fully in return. When he spoke again, the clipped, crisp tone of his voice had turned almost conversational. ''I'll take a rain check on the meal, but I don't think I'll be in the mood for chili for a while.''

As the man sauntered out of the diner, leaving behind a small trail of diced onions and peppers, Tess let out a sigh of relief. Not only was the man easy on the eye, but if his casual attitude about his ruined suit was any indication, he would be easy on her bank account as well.

Humming lightheartedly, she went in search of a mop.

A couple of hours later, Jack Maris had showered and given the offending clothes to the concierge at the Saint Sebastian in the hope that something might be salvaged.

Now that he had washed away the pungent scent of onions and chili pepper, Jack reclined on the room's queen-sized bed, stacked his hands behind his head on the pillow, and tried to ignore the angry growl of his empty stomach. He didn't want to bother with room service. His thoughts strayed to the waitress who had taken his order at the little hole-in-the-wall diner. He'd always been a sucker for long red hair, and the young woman with the gray eyes and full rosy lips had it in abundance. He recalled the way a few wisps of it had escaped the confines of the severe ponytail she wore, and he thought about the rather vivid fantasy he had been enjoying as he watched her walk to his table, her smoky gaze a mixture of awareness and uncertainty.

What would she do if I tugged that mass of fiery hair free and ran my fingers through it until it snaked down her back? Jack had been wondering. A dousing of chili, hot though it was, had cooled his ardor considerably. Then he had felt so foolish, standing in front of her covered in soup and still slightly aroused, that he had practically bitten off her head with his remarks. In truth, his foul mood had had little to do with the pretty waitress or the unfortunate mishap. Indeed, the accident had been the perfect cap to a lousy day, he decided, his thoughts turning to the job interview that had brought him to town.

Ira Faust of Faust Enterprises was looking for a vice president. More than just a vice president really, he was courting an investor. Someone who was willing to buy into his distributorship. Someone who would become the new head of Faust Enterprises when Ira finally retired. The man was pushing eighty, so Jack figured it wouldn't be long. In the meantime, he would learn the business and bide his time.

Opportunities like this didn't present themselves every day, especially for someone as young as Jack Maris. At thirty-two, Jack didn't doubt he could handle the responsibility of running a company. He had graduated top of his class at Northwestern University, where he had earned his BA and MBA, and he excelled at solving problems and turning deficits into profits. The past several years in the employ of others had reinforced his desire to be his own boss. He wanted—needed—to be the master of his destiny, the one calling the shots for a change.

A therapist might say his need for control came from his chaotic childhood, and Jack admitted privately, it could be true. His parents were divorced and rather nomadic, moving often and remarrying with nearly the same frequency. But whatever motive lay behind his goal, Faust Enterprises was exactly the type of company he wanted to own—solid, established, respected. It was relatively small, with just less than four hundred employees, but Jack saw plenty of room for growth with someone more aggressive at the helm. He felt he was just the man Faust needed, and, thanks to the tidy sum Grandmother Maris had left him, Jack had the money to invest. For some reason, however, he got the impression Ira Faust was not quite convinced.

Jack stared at the stuccoed ceiling and reviewed the meeting. It had started off well enough: firm handshake, plenty of eye contact. Ira had given Jack the speech about how Faust Enterprises remained a family operation despite the fact that he was the only Faust still employed there. Ira and his brother Evan had begun the business in the family garage nearly sixty years before. Evan had died a confirmed bachelor seven years ago. Ira and his wife, Cora, had been blessed with only one daughter, and she had died tragically in a car accident when she was twenty-six. *Family.* The older man must have used the word more than a dozen times during the interview, Jack mused.

If he had to put his finger on when the interview began to stall out, it would be right after Ira Faust asked Jack to tell him a bit about himself.

"You've got a very impressive background, Mr. Maris. Graduated with honors from Northwestern. And your references are outstanding. But tell me something about yourself that's not on your resumé," Ira coaxed, leaning forward over the wide mahogany desk. He folded a pair of large, blue-veined hands on the blotter and waited for Jack's reply.

Jack had told him the standard things: where he was born, what he saw as his strengths, different experiences that made him uniquely qualified for the job.

As an afterthought he threw in: "I'm single, in excellent health, and I love to golf. Since Michigan has more courses per capita than any other state, I figure I'm going to enjoy working on taking a couple of strokes off my handicap. Too bad the season is so short here."

Ira offered a polite smile in return, but if Jack had to pinpoint it, he would say that was when the older man's demeanor changed. Subtly, sure, but Ira seemed to be mentally crossing Jack off the list of contenders.

The phone on the nightstand began to ring, and he snatched it up. "Maris here."

"Hey, Jack, how did the interview go?" Davis Marx asked. He worked as Faust's personnel director and had got Jack the interview. The two men had first met in an economics class as freshmen at Northwestern. They had remained close friends over the years, despite living in different states. Jack had even been best man at Davis's wedding a few years earlier.

"I don't know," Jack replied. "I mean, it started out great, then it just fizzled. Funny thing is, I think I had him hooked until he asked me about my personal life."

"What the heck did you say?"

"Nothing outrageous. Basically I told him I'm not married, and I like to spend my spare time on a golf course. It's not as if I said, 'By the way, I deal drugs, don't believe in paying taxes, and belong to a militia group.'"

Davis groaned dramatically. "Don't you ever listen to me? I told you the man all but lives and dies by family. When he asked what you do in your spare time couldn't you have at least thrown in visits with your sister or parents?"

"But I haven't seen any of them in more than a year."

Davis groaned again. "I know, but couldn't you have stretched the truth? Or, better yet, hinted at a serious relationship with a woman? I told you Ira all but did backflips when I tied the knot. Yet you go in there and announce that you're single and probably gave him the impression you're not looking for a wife."

"I'm not," Jack said flatly.

"Yeah, and that's got Ira thinking, 'How committed will this guy be to the company I built from nothing when he can't even make a commitment to a woman?' Especially when your resumé seems to confirm his suspicions that you move around a lot. Three companies in five years. It doesn't exactly say steady as a rock, Jack."

"What do you suggest I do? Get married and have kids just to prove to the man that I'm stable and planning to put down roots here? I'm willing to invest a sizable sum of money in his company. Shouldn't that be enough of a commitment?"

"I'm not suggesting anything, and this conversation is strictly off the record, but I told you Faust is looking for a successor, a surrogate son of sorts who he can feel good about leaving in charge. Maybe it's not too late to make him think you're involved with someone. And I mean seriously involved, Jack, as in heading to the altar.''

"But I'm not involved. I told you, Nancy and I broke it off six months ago. And over this very issue.'' Jack thought about the woman back in Boston who had so recently shared his life, and felt a small prick of disappointment over their bitter parting after so many years of amicable co-existence. Yet, he couldn't keep the sneer from his voice when he added, "She wanted a ring, and she got one, just not from me. She's marrying the guy who sold her the Volvo.''

"Marriage isn't so bad, you know,'' Davis said quietly.

"I'm not saying it is,'' Jack insisted, scrubbing a hand over his prickly chin. "No one in my family has managed to make it work, although, God bless them, they just keep trying. But I know it does work for some people.'' His voice lowered a notch, sincerity replacing flippancy. "I'd say it works for you and Marianne, but it's just not in my long-range plans.''

"Well, you don't really have to get engaged,'' Davis said finally. "Just drop a few hints leaving that impression. Tell him your fiancée is back in Boston and won't be moving here until she wraps up loose ends. Once you have the job, it won't really matter. You can say things didn't work out. Look, Ira wants to see you again tomorrow morning. Officially, that's why I'm calling. Be in his office at ten o'clock sharp. Unofficially, I'm telling you that one little white lie really could help. Your call, Jack,'' he said before hanging up.

Jack mulled Davis's suggestion for the next couple of hours. He didn't like deceptions, but he wondered what one this small, this insignificant, could possibly hurt. He wasn't lying about his qualifications or keeping some vital piece of information to himself. His private life, after all, was no one's business but his own. Besides, he *did* plan to stick around if he got the position. When he became head of Faust, he planned to nurture and expand Ira's carefully built company, not slice it up and sell it off before he went on his merry way. His conscience duly wrestled into submission, he set the alarm clock and climbed under the covers.

Jack took several deep breaths, exhaling them slowly through his mouth in an effort to quell his nerves before the elevator reached its destination on the top floor at Faust. *Now or never, Maris,* he thought as he walked down the corridor to Ira's office. The receptionist smiled politely as Jack approached her cluttered desk.

"I'll let Mr. Faust know you're here, Mr. Maris," she told him.

"Jack, come in," Ira said a moment later. He held open his office door and waved Jack inside. "I hope it wasn't an inconvenience to come back today."

"Not at all, sir. I hope you'll excuse my casual attire." He motioned to the khaki trousers and navy sweater he wore beneath a leather jacket. "I only brought one suit, and, well, it had a little run-in with my dinner yesterday."

Ira chuckled as he settled into the chair behind his desk. "What you're wearing is fine. Shall we get down to business?"

Jack nodded and took a seat in one of the burgundy wing chairs that faced Ira's desk. For the next forty minutes they talked about Jack's work experience. Ira threw out several hypothetical situations and asked Jack how he would handle them. Again, Jack got the feeling the older man was impressed with him, but not quite sold. They were concluding their meeting when the lie that had been in the back of Jack's mind all morning popped out of his mouth.

"Well, it looks like I'll be able to make it for an early lunch with my fiancée after all," he said. Too disgusted with himself to make eye contact with Ira, Jack continued to stare at the gold watch strapped to his wrist.

He heard the leather of Ira's chair creak as the older man leaned forward. "Fiancée, you say?"

Jack nodded, his tongue unwilling to give voice to such a blatant untruth a second time.

"Ah, yes, better not keep the young woman waiting." Ira smiled brightly and Jack's stomach clenched. He considered retracting his words, but he told himself that one little fib wouldn't really matter.

Halfway to the door Ira laid a companionable hand on Jack's shoulder and confided, "I think you'll do nicely as the new vice president of Faust Enterprises. I'm offering you the position, with the option to invest in the company and then take over completely when I retire."

"That's terrific! I accept," he said, nearly sending up a whoop of joy that would have been entirely inappropriate for the vice president of a distributorship. More solemnly he added, "You won't regret this, sir."

"I'm sure I won't," Ira agreed. The two men shook hands, and Ira escorted Jack to the brass-doored elevator.

While they waited for the elevator to arrive, Ira said, "If you have no other plans for the evening, how about dinner? We can toast your new job, and I can answer any other questions you may have about either the company or the community. I'm sure Davis will help you with house-hunting, but I do know an excellent real estate agent if you're interested."

"That sounds great. I'd appreciate it."

The elevator arrived and Jack stepped inside, aware that he probably was wearing a silly grin on his face, but unable to check it. *Vice president*. He was the new vice president of Faust Enterprises, a company he would someday own as well as oversee. If possible, his grin widened.

"Then it's settled. My wife and I will meet you at your hotel at seven-thirty. The restaurant off the lobby serves an excellent rack of lamb," Ira replied, his own smile paternal and understanding.

The elevator's shiny doors were just beginning to slide shut when Ira added, "I'm looking forward to meeting your girl."

"He wants to meet my girl!" Jack thundered into the telephone.

"I can't believe you told him she was here," Davis replied, sounding incredulous. "Boston, Jack, she was supposed to be in Boston!"

"Yeah, well, forgive me for being a lousy liar. It just slipped out that way."

"Okay, okay, there's got to be a way to fix this," Davis muttered on the other end of the line.

Jack sighed miserably. "I have the position I've been dreaming about since graduate school, but the guy's probably going to rescind the offer as soon as he realizes I lied through my teeth to get it.'' He sank down on the edge of the bed and, with his free hand, kneaded the bunched muscles at the back of his neck.

''You could say she's not feeling well,'' Davis offered, then grunted skeptically. ''Of course, I wouldn't put it past Faust to show up at your hotel tomorrow with a doctor in tow. If he could just meet the future Mrs. Maris once, I'm sure that would be the end of it. Too bad you don't know any women willing to play the part of your happy bride-to-be. Unfortunately, most of the single women I know work at Faust, know someone at Faust, or wear support hose. But maybe Marianne has a friend. I'll call her at work.''

Jack stopped rubbing his neck and grinned as the idea hit him with the same force the crock of chili had the day before.

''Never mind that. I do know a woman,'' he said slowly. ''And as it happens, she owes me a huge favor.''

Chapter Two

Tess was on her afternoon break when she saw him walk into the restaurant. He was taller than she remembered, at least six-two, with broad shoulders and lean hips. She watched the other female diners swivel in their seats to give him the once-over as he passed their tables, and she smiled. With the body of an athlete and a face that belonged on the cover of *Gentleman's Quarterly,* he was a hard man to ignore.

Tess took a moment to hope he would sit in another waitress's section so that she would not have to face him again. She was surprised he had come back after yesterday's disaster. Her surprise turned to alarm when he continued to walk to the rear of the restaurant and to the table where she sat alone, eating chicken salad and reading a chapter on metropolitan government.

Oh God, she thought, nearly choking on her meal, *he's decided to make me pay after all.*

She was coughing when he reached her table. Her

eyes watered a little as the chicken salad finally went down with the help of a gulp of iced tea. Still wary, she studied his expression, but he didn't look angry or aggrieved. Nor was he holding a bill for a new suit. Instead, he smiled a little uncertainly and politely asked, "May I sit down?"

Heart hammering, Tess could do no more than bob her head in response.

"I'm assuming you remember me from yesterday," he said, sliding onto the seat opposite hers.

Oh yes, Tess thought, *I remember you.* He had the kind of face a woman would recall even if she had not also managed to humiliate herself so completely in his company.

"You do remember me?" he repeated. To her embarrassed dismay, Tess realized she had been staring at him like some infatuated adolescent.

"Um, yes, I remember you. I—I spilled chili in your lap. How is it by the way?"

His eyebrows shot up, and she clarified, "The suit, I mean, n-not your lap. Did the stain come out?"

Jack watched her blush again, as she had the day before, and he found it charming. Not many women blushed anymore, especially women who looked like this one. She wore her hair in a bun today, and once more he found himself wondering what it would look like when she let it down. To his guilty surprise, he began to fantasize again, picturing himself taking out the pins one at a time and watching thick curls the color of hot embers spill over her shoulders.

"Well, did it?" she asked, interrupting his fantasy.

He had to clear his throat twice before he could answer her question. "I haven't got the suit back from the cleaners yet, so I don't know if the stain came out.''

"Oh.''

He watched as some of the tension eased out of her shoulders, but the wariness remained in her gaze.

"I'm interrupting your lunch.'' He pointed to the half-eaten chicken salad on her plate.

"That's okay,'' she assured him. "I still have another fifteen minutes before I have to go back to work. Can I buy you a sandwich or something, to make up for yesterday?''

Jack smiled engagingly. He couldn't have asked for a better segue.

"As a matter of fact, there *is* something you can do for me. A favor, a *really* big favor,'' he stressed, leaning forward in his chair.

From across the table he watched the woman swallow nervously. "Wh-what sort of favor?''

"Nothing illegal, I promise. It's just that I've got myself into a jam. It's kind of humorous actually,'' he admitted with a rueful little chuckle. "I…um…led someone to believe I'm engaged. The only problem is, well, that's not quite true. But now he's asked my fiancée and me to dinner tonight.''

"The fiancée you don't have,'' she said, brows furrowed as she tried to follow his story.

"Yeah, that's right. So, I find myself in the odd predicament of needing a woman.'' As he said it, his gaze dropped to her mouth. Generous lips that were naturally rose-colored curved into an embarrassed smile, and he rethought his choice of words. "What I mean to say is, I need a woman to *act* as my fiancée.''

"And this involves me how, exactly?'' she asked,

but gauging from her expression, Jack could tell she had guessed and was struggling with whether she should be appalled or flattered.

"Will you do me the honor of being my fiancée for the evening?" he asked in solemn good humor.

Tilting her head to one side, she regarded him for a long moment. "You said this was nothing illegal."

He nodded.

"And it's just for the evening, right?"

"Just for the evening."

"Well, I'm working late, so I won't get off until seven," she told him, and Jack let out a relieved sigh. She hadn't exactly consented, but then she hadn't told him to get lost either. He decided to go on the assumption that since she was telling him what time she got off work, she was agreeing to his wacky plan.

"Hmm, seven." He rubbed a hand over his chin and did some quick calculations in his head. "That will be tight, but it could work. Dinner's at seven-thirty in the restaurant at the Saint Sebastian Hotel."

Jack heard the woman whistle through her teeth, but he was too excited to wonder at her reaction.

"I have a rental car," he said, his voice low and conspiratorial. "I could come pick you up here and you could freshen up in my hotel suite if you'd like."

He hadn't even finished speaking when she began shaking her head. "Look, I'd really like to help you out, but I don't have a thing to wear to a fancy place like that. The Saint Sebastian is easily the nicest place in town."

"But if you had a dress to wear, you'd go, right?"

"I suppose," she shrugged. "But I really can't afford to buy a new one right now, even if I had the time to go shopping. I'm sorry," she sighed with genuine regret, and said again, "I really would like to help you out."

Jack remained silent for a moment, then gave in to impulse. "Leave the dress to me."

"Oh no." She held up a hand and shook her head in protest. "I can't allow you to buy me a dress."

"Why not?"

"First of all, after what happened yesterday I'm the one who's supposed to be doing you the favor, remember?"

"So? You'd still be doing me a favor. If it helps, think of the dress as a prop that I'll supply and that you get to keep afterward," he suggested with a smile.

"But I hardly even know you," she sputtered. Then, "I don't even know your name!"

"That's easy enough to remedy. It's Jack. Jack Q. Maris. The Q is for Quinten." He squinted at her in mock challenge. "I don't tell many people that because I hate the name, but I tend to make exceptions for close friends and pseudo-fiancées."

When she just sat there and stared at him as if he had grown two heads, he prompted, "And you are?"

"Oh! I'm Tess. Officially, Tessa Claire Donovan, but nobody calls me Tessa," she added, narrowing her eyes in much the same way he had.

Jack held out his hand and waited until she extended one of her own. He clasped the slender hand tightly and, for the third time since he had first seen her, he watched Tess blush.

"It's nice to finally meet you." Still holding her hand, he added, "By the power vested in me by the state of desperation, I now pronounce you, Tessa Claire Donovan, my make-believe fiancée."

* * *

Tess stood outside Earl's Place, shoulders hunched against the crisp November evening. She had managed to clock out fifteen minutes early and to change into the jeans and cotton blouse she'd worn to work that morning, and she was hoping Jack would be as good as his word and arrive on time. She still couldn't believe she had agreed to go to dinner with him, much less pose as his fiancée for the evening. What did she know about the man, after all, except that he had the most gorgeous green eyes, a sexy smile, and a body that seemed chiseled from rock? For all she knew he could be some deranged madman loose from a psychiatric ward, or a serial rapist stalking his next victim.

But then she remembered the way he'd said her name, wrapping his tongue around that one simple syllable as if he were savoring it. And she recalled the way a mere handshake had stolen her breath. To herself, she admitted that even if yesterday's mishap had not compelled her to agree to help him, she would be waiting outside Earl's Place anyway. The man intrigued her. And her unprecedented reaction to him intrigued the practical, unflappable Tess even more.

"You need a ride, Tess?" one of the regulars asked on his way out of the restaurant.

"Thanks, but no, my date should be here any minute," she replied. She smiled after she said it. *My fiancé*, she corrected silently, then allowed herself the indulgence of a fantasy. She pictured a shiny white limousine pulling to the curb, a black-capped chauffeur stepping out to open the door for her. Inside, Jack sat on supple leather seats holding out a flute of champagne, his smile warm with promise. Tess gave herself a mental shake as Jack's tan rental sedan pulled to the curb. What was wrong with her? This was no date. It was playacting, two people pretending to be intimately acquainted and doing it for a small, exclusive audience. She pushed aside the sharp twinge of disappointment she felt and concentrated on the evening ahead.

A thought occurred to her as they headed down Fifth Street to the Saint Sebastian. "Jack, if we're supposed to be engaged, shouldn't I know more about you than just your name?"

"Good point. Let's see, I graduated from Northwestern University with a degree in accounting. That's also where I got my master's in business administration." He gave her his full attention while they waited for a traffic light to change. "I was born in Chicago. My father moved back to the Windy City a couple of years ago. My mom's in Aspen, and I have one older sister, Kirsten, who's rather nomadic, but she's living in California these days. I've been living in Boston and working for a company there."

The light turned green and the car pulled forward.

"Should I be from Boston, too?" she asked.

He thought a minute, then shook his head. "No, I think you should be from Chicago. You have a Midwest accent."

She shrugged, taking his word for it, although she had never considered herself to have an accent of any sort.

"Okay, so how did we meet if you live in Boston?"

"Hmm. How old are you?" he asked, glancing sideways.

"Twenty-four."

He pursed his lips. "Well, that pretty much rules out college. How about, we met when I went home to visit family a few years ago, and we've maintained a long-distance relationship ever since, waiting for you to finish college and me to find my dream job before we settled down."

It sounded rather romantic to Tess, and much more exciting than her own boring life, but she replied in a bland voice, "I guess that's plausible." She couldn't resist asking, "Just how old are you?"

"I'm not robbing-the-cradle old," he insisted with a throaty chuckle that had her smiling in return. She liked the sound of his laughter, and the easy camaraderie that had sprung up between them.

"Just how old is 'not robbing-the-cradle old'?" she asked.

"I'm only thirty-two."

"Thirty-two, huh?" She gave him a quick once-over and said, "Looking at you, I'd have to say you've aged remarkably well." The teasing tone of her voice sounded flirtatious even to her own ears. It wasn't like her to flirt. In fact, she hadn't realized she knew how. The man certainly had an odd effect on her. When he glanced curiously in her direction, Tess busied herself rummaging through her purse for some breath mints.

They arrived at the hotel five minutes later and bustled inside. While they waited for the elevator, Jack spared a glance in the direction of the restaurant.

"Well, it doesn't appear our dinner companions have arrived yet," he said, sounding relieved. As they stepped into the elevator, they continued to discuss their bogus courtship.

A minute later, the elevator reached the seventh

floor. When the double doors slid open, the easy banter they had been sharing evaporated along with the saliva in Tess's mouth. As she waited for him to unlock the door to his room, she looked anxiously up and down the corridor, half expecting someone she knew to pop out and ask her what she was doing going into a strange man's hotel room. The hall remained empty, but she couldn't quite shake the feeling that she was doing something illicit, especially when Jack finally managed to open the door to his room and stood at the threshold waiting for her. She brushed past him, feeling awkward and foolish, but then she spied the dress he had laid ever so carefully across the bed's floral comforter and her mouth fell open.

"You said size six, right?" He stood just behind her, and she could swear she felt his warm breath feather across the nape of her neck when he spoke.

"Six, yes," she repeated, transfixed. Basic and black, it was easily the most elegant dress Tess had ever seen. It reminded her a bit of the sleek number Audrey Hepburn had worn in *Breakfast at Tiffany's.* She heard a wistful sigh, and realized it was her own. She adored Audrey Hepburn, but she especially loved her in that movie. It was as if he had known, she thought, then chided herself for being silly. They were strangers, after all. He barely knew her name, let alone what old movies she preferred.

But the man had taste; she would say that for him. She had spent the afternoon agonizing over what kind of a dress he would pick out for her to wear. Would it be sleazy or too prim? Would it be in some horrendous shade that would clash with her flaming hair? But Jack had chosen well.

She decided he must have driven over to the mall in Piedmont during the afternoon. Pleasant River certainly didn't have any place that carried such stylish evening dresses. She spied the label stitched just inside the neckline and, limited though her exposure to designer fashions was, she knew it must have cost him a mint.

"The lady at the store helped me pick it out," he said. "Um, she also helped pick out the, uh, other things." He coughed a little self-consciously, and for the first time Tess noticed the lacy black slip and sheer hose lying next to the dress on the bed.

"Oh," was all she could manage, grateful he stood behind her and could not watch her face redden.

"The shoes were a little trickier. I hope they're comfortable." His tone was dubious.

Tess noticed the pair of strappy black leather heels lined up at the foot of the bed next to a pair of size-eleven men's dress shoes. For some reason the sight of their footwear sharing space next to a bed seemed more intimate than the fact the man had helped pick out her unmentionables.

"Well, everything seems to be in order," he said, rubbing his hands together. He walked to the closet and pulled out a new suit. It was double-breasted and the color of charcoal, with the barest hint of a pin-stripe. She noticed the tags still dangling from the cuff. At her questioning gaze, he offered a careless shrug.

"The chili didn't come out. I guess you could say my American Express card got quite the workout today, especially since I had to have them do a rush job on the alterations."

She opened her mouth to speak, but he held up a

hand to forestall the apology that she was about to offer. "Don't say you're sorry, Tess. After tonight, we're more than even."

"Okay," she agreed. "I won't apologize. But can I say thank you?"

He grinned, that sexy little dimple tugging in his cheek. "You're welcome. Now we'd better get ready. I can change in the bathroom, unless you'd like to freshen up first?"

"Yes, please. I think I smell like chili dogs." She crinkled her nose. "I'll just take the dress and the other things in there with me," she told him, quickly gathering them up. "I won't be long."

Jack glanced at his watch. "I hate to rush you, but it's almost twenty after," he said.

Jack Maris had never known a woman who could be ready in five minutes. Nancy and her endless fussing over her appearance had caused them to be chronically late.

He changed into his suit and paced the length of the room once. Then he went to the closed bathroom door and raised his hand to knock, planning to tell Tess he would meet her downstairs. He didn't want to keep his new partner waiting. The door opened before he could knock, however, and Jack's eyes widened at the sight that greeted him.

"Ready," she announced. She gave her head a little shake that sent copper-colored curls dancing.

He sucked in a sharp breath. None of the fantasies he'd had about her hair matched the reality. It corkscrewed nearly to her waist in rivulets of molten lava.

"I took down my hair," she said needlessly when

he kept staring at it. "I can put it back up. I just thought—"

"No, no," he interrupted her, his voice a little gruff. "Leave it down. It's..." Then Jack noticed the dress. The woman whose firm curves filled it out so nicely needed no flounces, ruffles or sequins to compensate for—or camouflage—any shortcomings. Perfection, he thought, as his heart picked up speed. She was sheer perfection.

"Tess. I..." His voice trailed away along with his train of thought, and whatever he had been about to say was swallowed up by the awkwardness of the moment.

He watched as color suffused her face. She seemed to look everywhere in the room but at him, and Jack wondered what had possessed him to stand there gawking at her as if he were some pimply-faced schoolboy on a first date. This wasn't a date at all, he reminded himself, although it was difficult to ignore the sexual attraction that had his blood heating.

Finally, his tone crisp and businesslike to compensate for the erotic thoughts he'd been entertaining, he said, "Come on, let's go get this over with."

Tess followed Jack through the beveled-glass doors of the Saint Sebastian's dining room and looked around. With the exception of an older couple seated near the rear of the restaurant, most of the faces were unfamiliar. Most likely out-of-town guests, she decided, wondering who she and Jack were there to meet. She smiled at the diners seated at each table they approached, eager to look the part of a happy bride-to-be, but Jack just kept walking. He walked past the young couple enjoying linguini in the booth near the wall. Past the dark-suited businessman scribbling notes on a yellow pad of paper. Past the trio of middle-aged women sipping coffee and eating cheesecake. That's when she knew, and her stomach felt as if it had dropped to her feet. She snagged Jack by the arm and tugged him to a halt.

"Wh-what is it?" he asked.

"The Fausts," she replied in a hushed tone. "You didn't tell me we were eating dinner with Ira and Cora Faust."

His eyes widened as his face bleached of color. "Please tell me you don't know them."

"Everyone in Pleasant River knows them," she whispered frantically. "They're the city's first family, so to speak. They sponsor just about everything that goes on around here, from the Christmas pageant to the annual blueberry festival. I was Miss Blueberry twice in high school. Ira Faust crowned me, for heaven's sake!"

At any other time, Jack thought, he might have been amused by the quaint image her words brought to mind, but with the beginning of a nasty headache pounding behind his eyes, he could only groan. Briefly, he considered turning around and slinking out. Later he could make up some excuse. But Ira took away that option by calling out, "Look, dear, here they are."

Jack sent Tess a pleading look, then plastered a smile on his face as they joined the Fausts at their table.

"Good evening, sir. Sorry to have kept you waiting." He turned to the plump, silver-haired matron who was seated next to Ira and said, "This must be your lovely wife. It's a pleasure to meet you, ma'am."

Any hope he harbored that the older couple would not recognize his date was dashed immediately.

"Why, this *is* a surprise," Cora Faust said, her tone incredulous and a little excited. "Don't tell me that Pleasant River's very own Tess Donovan is your fiancée?"

"Young man, why didn't you mention that your girl was a local?" Ira admonished good-naturedly. "This is extraordinary."

"Hello, Mr. Faust," Tess said. Jack noticed her discreetly wiping her palm on her dress before shaking the older man's hand. Turning to Ira's wife, she said, "It's good to see you again, Mrs. Faust."

They were seated, and the waiter came for their drink order, forestalling what Jack knew was only the inevitable. Tess ordered a club soda, apparently determined to keep a clear head. Jack, however, ordered Scotch. False courage, he decided, was better than nothing. The black-vested server had barely moved out of hearing range when Cora lobbed the first verbal volley of what promised to be a long evening of probing questions.

"Tess, dear, I ran into your mother just last month at the beauty shop. We chatted while I was waiting for my manicure to dry. She never mentioned your engagement. When exactly did this occur?"

"Um, well, actually…" Tess turned to Jack, her gaze silently beseeching him to clear up this misunderstanding before it went any further.

For the millionth time, he wondered why he had listened to Davis's foolish suggestion, even as he admitted that the plan had worked splendidly. He had the job. And, God help him, he wanted to keep it. Below the folds of the linen tablecloth he reached for Tess's hand, offering a reassuring squeeze, and sent her a look that begged for understanding.

"It happened rather suddenly. In fact, we haven't told our families yet. We wanted it to be secret, just for a little while longer. I'm sure you can understand that." His gaze strayed to Cora and he winked at the older woman, as if including her in some Shakespearean plot. Cora's eyes misted, evidence, Jack decided, of her romantic heart. He felt himself relax a bit.

"Oh, of course. Ira and I were young once. I remember how love was at the beginning. Not that it's not still wonderful after all these years, but at first it's all…" she seemed to hunt for the right word, then, she sighed, "…magic."

"This calls for a toast," Ira announced, giving Jack an affectionate thump on the back. The waiter had just arrived with their drinks, but as he transferred them from the tray to the table, Ira said, "Any proper toast must be done with champagne."

The waiter returned and was filling their glasses with sparkling wine when Cora said, "Where on earth did you two kids meet? Ira tells me you're from Boston, Jack. When did Tess take a trip to Boston?"

The tale they had concocted in the car clearly no longer applied.

"That's actually a very interesting story, isn't it Tess?" Jack began, buying time. Tess nodded vigorously, and he watched her gulp down champagne, nearly emptying the fluted glass before she returned it to the table. Apparently she also needed a little false courage now. Always one to oblige a woman in distress, he reached over to refill her glass.

"You were saying," Cora prompted helpfully.

"Um, yes, how Tess and I met. It's a very interesting story," he repeated inanely. His mind, however, remained stubbornly blank. Ira and Cora Faust seemed to lean forward in their seats, as if willing the words out of his mouth, but no matter how fast his brain searched for a scenario they would believe, nothing came. It was no use, he decided. He sent Tess an apologetic little smile and opened his mouth, ready to expose his idiotic deception and beg the Fausts' pardon.

"The truth is—"

That's all he got out before Tess interrupted.

"It was last spring."

Jack watched her swallow thickly as she realized she had the Fausts' undivided attention. They regarded her with polite curiosity, while he had the feeling his own expression held a mixture of gratitude and panicky desperation.

Tess drained the rest of her champagne, stalling shamelessly as she searched her imagination for some plausible explanation. She couldn't believe she was going to lie, and not just some lie of omission either, but a whopper elaborate enough to satisfy the town's pre-eminent busybody. A painting hung on the wall behind Cora, a gilt-framed watercolor of a basket of fresh-cut lilies. It gave her an idea.

"Uh, Jack and I met at the French Impressionists exhibit at the Detroit Institute of Art. We're both huge fans of Monet."

Tess smiled in relief. She had gone to the exhibit alone, so no one would be able to prove or disprove her story. The Fausts and Jack seemed to be waiting for her to continue, so she did, surprised by how easily it all came to her as one falsehood after another slipped from her lips, transforming her staid, predictable life into something to sigh over.

"Um, we, uh, corresponded for months afterward. And talked on the telephone a lot, too. But it was through his letters that I fell in love with him." She sent Jack a shy smile that had Cora Faust's ample bosom heaving in appreciation.

Tess was thinking about the love letters the star-crossed Abelard and Héloïse had sent to one another in the twelfth century. She had studied them in a history class during her freshman year of college. They were beautiful letters, full of passion and heartache and unbearable longing. She had read them with a box of tissues at her side; her heart breaking for two lovers who had remained true to one another despite the horrendous circumstances that forced them apart forever. She wanted a love as pure as that—minus the tragedy, of course.

Tess smiled at Cora and confided, "You get to know a lot about a man by how well he can put his thoughts down on paper."

"So when's the big day?" Ira asked.

"We haven't set a date yet," Jack responded at the same time that Tess, still caught up in the romantic fantasy she'd been concocting, replied rather dreamily, "June."

They stared at one another in stricken silence as Ira and Cora looked on in amusement.

"Women always want June weddings, my boy," Ira said, nodding sagely. "Marriage is about compromise. They demand and we bend." He added a sly wink when his wife slapped his arm. "Might as well start by compromising on the wedding date."

"I'll think about it, sir," he mumbled, trading champagne for a bracing gulp of Scotch.

The waiter returned for their dinner orders and, for the time being they were spared having to devise any more creative responses. For the next twenty minutes Jack managed to steer the conversation back to Faust Enterprises and his new responsibilities there. But when their entrées arrived, Cora routed the conversation once again to matrimony by exclaiming, "My goodness, dear, where is your engagement ring?"

She captured Tess's hand and held it up to her myopic eyes for inspection.

"Oh…well," Tess sputtered.

"Honey," Jack tsk-ed. "You must have left it next to the bathroom sink in our suite."

Tess smothered a groan while Cora's mouth puckered into a shocked O.

"You're staying in his hotel room?" the older woman asked in a scandalized voice, holding a hand to her bosom.

Tess wanted to die. The sexual revolution might have taken place decades ago, but a woman like Cora Faust, who donned white gloves on Sunday and probably still wore a corset, didn't hold with co-habitation before marriage. What had Jack been thinking, giving the woman the impression that he and Tess were physically intimate? Tess pictured Cora and the other ladies at Mabel's Style Haven discussing Tess's sleeping arrangements as they sat under the dryers, and she knew if her mother caught wind of this, Rita Donovan wouldn't need a permanent to put curl in her hair.

"N-n-no, ma'am," she stuttered, offering a prim smile as she fidgeted in her seat like a first-grader caught eating paste. "I got off work at seven, and it was easier to come straight here and get ready upstairs than to drive all the way home and wait for Jack to come pick me up there."

That much, at least, was the truth. And while Cora nodded, Tess had the feeling the cagey older woman wasn't completely convinced of Tess's chastity.

It was almost ten when the waiter brought the check, and Tess left the restaurant on shaking limbs, unable to clearly remember all of the lies she and Jack had spun for the Fausts' benefit. All she knew for certain was that she had started out the day worried about a midterm exam and ended it with the town's most celebrated gossip believing she was engaged to, and carnally involved with the gorgeous new vice president of Faust Enterprises.

Tess had traded black silk for denim and cotton, and sat huddled in the front seat of Jack's rental car waiting for the heat to kick in as they drove back to Earl's Place. Beside her Jack groaned and muttered, "I can't believe I let it get this far."

He'd been saying basically the same thing since leaving the Fausts, but this time Tess felt the need to offer her own bit of editorial comment.

"You? My reputation is in tatters. Cora Faust thinks we've been..." she gestured wildly with her hand to fill in the blank. Just thinking the words made her uncomfortable. She couldn't bring herself to say them aloud.

"We've been what?" Jack asked. He turned toward her, and she saw the beginnings of a smile tugging at the corners of his mouth.

"You know only too well what she thinks we've

been doing," Tess croaked. They passed the beauty shop, where gossip was dispensed as freely as the hairspray, and something even more depressing occurred to her. "What if this gets back to my mother? I'm twenty-four, but I may as well be in pinafores as far as my mother is concerned."

He sent her a sympathetic look before returning his attention to the road.

"On the bright side, at least the man you're supposedly sleeping with is willing to make an honest woman out of you." When he glanced her way, Tess sent him a withering look intended to tell him exactly what she thought of his attempt at humor.

"Sorry. Just trying to lighten the mood."

But Tess didn't want her mood lightened. She slumped against the headrest and closed her eyes. "What if my family learns of our supposed engagement?" she moaned.

"Maybe they won't get wind of it. Maybe Cora will keep quiet for a while out of a sense of romance, and by the time she says anything to your family, this entire mess will be resolved. Then you can tell them the truth and have a good laugh over it."

"Somehow, I doubt they would find this funny."

Jack brought the car to a stop in the lot behind Earl's Place and shifted into park. He turned to face her and when he spoke, all humor was gone from his voice.

"I'm really sorry, Tess. I didn't mean to drag you so deeply into my predicament."

The street lamp illuminated only half of his face, but there was no mistaking his sincerity. She exhaled slowly and straightened in her seat. "Oh, it's not all your fault. I went along with it, even when I realized who we were supposed to be fooling. I could have said no, but I didn't.''

''Why did you do it?'' he asked softly, his gaze just a little too direct.

Tess looked away. She didn't have an answer for him, not one she could share without sounding pathetic. How could she tell him that work and school had taken up so much of her life for the past several years that she hadn't had time for many dates or much fun? And despite all the complications their ''date'' had wrought, she had had fun. She'd enjoyed putting on a sexy dress and going out to a fancy restaurant. She'd enjoyed Jack's company and the forbidden feelings he conjured up in her whenever he smiled or touched her hand. It was heady stuff for a woman who spent most of her spare time dressed in ratty sweats, her nose pressed into a textbook.

''Tess?'' he prompted.

She decided it was best to ignore the question. ''I can't believe I said we're having a June wedding. It just got out of control.''

''Yeah,'' Jack said with a sigh. He leaned his forehead on the steering wheel and moaned like a man facing amputation without anesthesia. ''Way out of control. I guess we should own up to it and apologize. We probably should have done that from the start. It would have been much easier.''

''I've been thinking the same thing myself, although I don't relish the thought of telling Cora Faust I lied to her.'' In jest, she asked, ''Got any other ideas?''

Jack rolled his head to the side on the steering wheel and squinted at her, as if taking her question seriously. ''Well, we could keep up the charade for a little while longer. I mean, just long enough for my position to be secure. Then we could tell the Fausts we called off our engagement.'' He sat up and shrugged. ''Tell them we decided we just weren't suited.''

''Jack, I don't know. My family.''

''I'm asking a lot, I know. Before you say no, think about it. We've already asked the Fausts to keep our engagement a secret. We could also ask them to keep quiet about our breakup to spare us any public embarrassment. No one else needs ever know we lied.'' He grinned triumphantly. ''It's a brilliant plan, Tess.''

''You mean devious.''

''Well,'' he cocked his head to one side. ''Maybe just a little, but my intentions, ultimately, aren't dishonest.''

She remained quiet for a moment, surprised to find she was actually considering what he proposed.

''It wouldn't be for long, Tess, I promise. A few weeks, maybe a month. What do you say?''

Tess glanced around the empty parking lot and tried to figure out just why she was willing to continue playing along with this scheme, because that's precisely what she was prepared to do. Surely, she had more than paid Jack back for the ruined suit. But then, Tess knew it had stopped being about the suit several lies ago. Maybe it had never been about the suit at all.

She liked Jack Maris. She liked spending time with him. She liked the way he said her name, and the way he had held her hand as they sat at the table, stroking the pad of his thumb over her knuckles with such casual tenderness. Maybe she was just being a fool, but this—whatever *this* was—felt right. She thought about her mother's firm belief in fate. Perhaps Tess should believe in such things herself.

"I must be crazy," she muttered.

Jack's brows pulled together. "Is that a yes?"

"Yes, I'll do it," she said slowly.

In the low light, he looked relieved, then oddly troubled, as if he were having second thoughts. Fiddling with his seat belt, he said, "Make sure, Tess. You don't have to, you know. I may have made you feel obligated, but you're not."

"It's just a white lie, really," she said, trying to reassure him as well as herself.

"Right, just one little white lie. Who can it hurt?"

"Certainly not the Fausts," she agreed a little desperately. "After all, how can our pretending to be engaged possibly hurt them?"

"It will just be one less gift for them to buy come June," he added with a smile.

"Then it's settled."

Once they reached an agreement there seemed little reason not to say good-night, but Tess hesitated until the silence became awkward.

"Well, I..." she said at the same time Jack began to speak. They both laughed a little tightly, then she said, "Go on, please."

"I was just going to say that I'm flying back to Boston on Sunday night. I need to pack up my things and get my affairs in order." He pulled a business card from his wallet and scribbled something on the back before handing it to her. "Here's a number where you can reach me in the evenings if anything comes up. If you need me before Sunday call me at the Saint Sebastian."

She nodded and tucked the card inside her purse.

"Well, I suppose I had better get going. I have a test tomorrow night that I haven't studied for yet."

"Test?"

She beamed a smile in his direction and informed him grandly, "Your fiancée, Jack Maris, is a college student, who, after this semester, will be only twelve credits shy of a degree in journalism."

"Really?"

"Really. What did you think, that my aspirations stopped at being a waitress at Earl's Place?"

Tess's words held only teasing humor, but Jack realized he didn't know what she aspired to be. He didn't know much about her at all except that she had gorgeous hair, filled out a size-six dress with the perfection of a fashion model, and blushed prettily with only the slightest provocation. But those were superficial things. He surprised himself by wanting to know more about Tess Donovan. Much more.

She opened the door and got out, then poked her head back inside the car. The heavy curtain of her hair dangled down with all the invitation of a bullfighter's cape. He wondered if she realized how sexy she was, and decided that she didn't when the smile she offered was more shy than sensual.

"Thank you for a very memorable evening, Jack."

"Memorable," he murmured as he watched her walk away.

Chapter Three

Dawn had barely broken the next morning when Jack donned sweats and set out on a five-mile run. The Saint Sebastian's bellhop had mapped out the route and assured Jack it was scenic. Jack didn't care about scenery. He wanted to clear his head, and he generally found that a punishing run helped him do that. These days he had a lot mucking up his orderly life.

The brisk pace he'd set had his quad muscles burning mercilessly after just two miles. That's when he spotted Tess in the park. She had braided her hair into a tidy, thick rope that hung down her back, but there was no mistaking that bright flash of color. Then he noticed what she was wearing: a faded Michigan State University sweatshirt over a pair of black tights. She was using a park bench to stretch out her legs, first one and then the other, and Jack felt his heart rate spike well past his targeted zone.

"Hey!" he wheezed, fighting for oxygen. "Tess!"

She looked up and squinted in the gray morning light, then she smiled, recognizing him. When he stopped at her side she said, "This is a surprise. I didn't know you jogged."

"Yep." He huffed out the one syllable before his breathing evened out enough to add, "I try to do five miles at least three times a week. What about you?"

"I'm a walker. No running for me. Bad for the knees," she explained, gesturing in their direction. Even encased in black, he thought they were nice knees.

He rested his hands on his hips. "How far do you go?"

"I try to walk three miles on Mondays, Wednesdays, and Fridays before I start work. That way I can sleep in and enjoy my weekends without feeling guilty." She pointed down the path that paralleled the river. "Want to walk with me for a while? I'm kind of on a tight schedule."

"Sure."

They walked in companionable silence for almost a quarter mile. Her speed surprised Jack. Those long legs of hers ate up the distance, forcing him to move briskly to keep up.

"You walk this pace for three miles?" he asked, impressed.

She angled him a cocky grin and replied, "No, I speed up after the first mile. I try to keep a twelve-minute-mile pace. That way I have plenty of time to shower and get ready for work. Earl has a little shower in the back office that he lets me use on the mornings I walk."

"Why not walk in your own neighborhood?"

"It's not as pretty as this." She motioned to the

river next to the path, its lazy current taking it past trees whose leaves had long since withered to a rusty brown and dropped to the ground. The limbs that might have flowered in spring or borne fruit in summer were now adorned with only an occasional bird's nest. Jack wasn't one to notice such things usually, but he did as he and Tess strode companionably along.

They were well into mile number two when he said, "You mind if I ask you something personal?"

She shrugged her shoulders. "I guess not, seeing as how we're engaged and all."

"Why aren't you going to school full-time instead of working at Earl's Place? You could get your degree sooner." He had thought about it last night after he had dropped her off, wondering why someone as bright and ambitious as she appeared to be hadn't already gotten her diploma.

"I know, but I can't afford tuition if I'm not earning a paycheck."

"Surely your folks would help you out."

She shook her head. "It's just my mom now, and she's living on a rather fixed income. My father died unexpectedly. They didn't have life insurance or much in the way of savings. Mom's got all she can handle just trying to keep her own bills paid."

"Sorry about your dad. When did he pass away?"

"Six years ago. I was a senior in high school at the time. I'd planned to go away to college. I had a scholarship to Michigan State," she said, plucking at the faded green and white sweatshirt she wore. Then she shrugged. "Life happens, you know? I couldn't leave my mother. My older sister, Betsy, had already gotten married and moved out. Mom needed me."

She made it sound so simple, as if her decision had cost her nothing. Perhaps she didn't feel it had, Jack realized, but he recognized the sacrifices she had made, and he respected her for them. He doubted any of the people in his family would have put their own happiness on hold under similar circumstances. As far as he could tell, the Maris family motto had always been: "Look out for Number One."

"You still live at home then?"

"No. Mom sold the house last year and bought a smaller one near Betsy. I moved into an apartment, which is another reason I can't afford to take a full load of classes." She lifted her shoulders. "I'll graduate eventually."

"I don't doubt that. It's important to you."

"Very. It's what I've always wanted. My dad..." she halted midsentence, sending him an embarrassed smile. "I'm sure you don't want to hear all of this."

"Your dad what?"

She hesitated a moment, as if gauging his sincerity. Then, "Well, my dad always said I'd be a great reporter. He said I asked more questions than ten children."

"Is that why you want to be a journalist? Because of your dad?"

"In part." She was quiet for a moment, and he thought that might be all the answer she intended to give. She'd stepped up her pace, too. Long legs stretching out, slender arms pumping determinedly. They'd walked half a mile before Tess finally spoke again, and when she did, her quiet words surprised Jack.

"I don't want to end up like my mom. Don't get me wrong," she said quickly, gray eyes beseeching him to understand. "My mother is terrific, wonderful. She's the best mom in the world, as far as I'm concerned. But I've seen how hard these past six years have been for her. She's got a high-school diploma and before Dad died, she hadn't worked outside the home in more than twenty years. She's had a tough time finding a good-paying job, and the one she has now offers few benefits. I guess I want more security. A college degree and a career doing something I enjoy would offer some, so I will not settle for less."

"That's understandable, and I'll bet your mother wants it for you, too," he replied, thinking she certainly was independent and driven—two attributes he'd never cared much for in a woman, and yet neither seemed to detract from Tess's femininity or that aura of vulnerability that surrounded her.

They walked a few minutes in silence, then she stopped. "Well, I think this is where we part company."

He could see the sign for Earl's Place in the distance, but Tess was pointing to the left. "If you follow that street to the next intersection and turn right, it will take you back to the park. I'm afraid you'll have quite a jog back to the Saint Sebastian, though."

"That's okay. The run will do me good. I've got a lot on my mind these days." He flashed a wolfish grin. "I'm not sure how it happened since I've managed thirty-two years without making a permanent commitment to a woman, but rumor has it I'm engaged."

"I've heard that rumor." She walked backward a few paces, her head tilted flirtatiously. "Lucky woman." With that she turned and hurried away.

Jack stood in the middle of the sidewalk and

watched her go, a smile warming his lips. She kept up the same brisk pace for the two blocks it took her to reach the restaurant, and his gaze followed the gentle sway of her hips the entire way.

Saturday mornings were for relaxation, as far as Jack was concerned. He was stretched out on the bed in his hotel room, reading the *Wall Street Journal* and sipping his third cup of coffee when the telephone rang. He was expecting Davis to call. The two of them had plans to look at a couple of houses that afternoon. But the voice he heard through the receiver was female and very agitated.

"Jack, I'm so glad I caught you!"

"Tess? Hey, what's wrong? You sound upset."

"We've got a little crisis," she replied in a thin voice.

He pinched the bridge of his nose between his thumb and index finger and bit back a sigh. "What's happened now?"

"Cora Faust apparently mentioned our engagement to the manicurist at the beauty shop yesterday, and now the news is spreading like wildfire."

"Great," he sighed, silently cursing the effectiveness of a small town's grapevine.

"My sister called last night, livid, I might add, that I had not confided in her that I was seriously involved with someone. I had barely hung up when my mother called."

"Oh, no," he groaned.

"Oh, yes. After hollering at me for half an hour because she had to hear about this from the lady who does her hair, she started to cry. She was so hurt that I had not introduced the two of you yet." Tess's voice hitched. "Gosh, Jack, she thinks I'm ashamed of her."

"Aw, Tess. I never meant to drag you and your family into this." He took a deep breath. "It's just not worth it. I'm going to call Ira Faust and tell him everything."

"No!"

"No? Tess, it's tearing your family apart. I can't stand by and let that happen. What kind of a man do you think I am?"

"What time is your flight tomorrow?" she asked.

He wasn't quite sure what to make of her switch in topics, but he answered anyway. "Six in the evening. Why?"

"Can you come for Sunday dinner at my sister's house around two?" Before he could reply she rushed ahead. "I had hoped news of our engagement wouldn't get back to them. But there's no helping it now. Jack, my family wants to meet my fiancé. And...and I think it's best that's who they think you are."

"What? Are you crazy? I think we should at least tell *them* the truth."

"Why, so they can lie, too? No, I'd rather not involve them. Besides, my mother would never be able to intentionally mislead Cora Faust. It's better this way."

Taking his make-believe fiancée to meet his new partner was one thing, but deceiving her family had a cold sweat trickling down his spine. Jack wondered if they would be able to fool the people who knew and loved Tess. If they couldn't, he realized, the entire thing would unravel. But he wasn't the only one who had something to lose now. For Tess, the trust and respect of her family were on the line.

"Are you sure you want to do this?"

"I gave you my word," she said simply. "The lies have been told already. There's no untelling them at this point without hurting a lot of people. It's just a matter of a few weeks," she said, almost to herself. But the relative brevity of the situation didn't make Jack feel better.

Tess lived upstairs in a stately older home that had been converted into two apartments. From the window of her small living room, she watched Jack park his car at the curb. He got out, wearing the same khaki trousers and navy sweater he'd had on the day he'd pretended to propose. Had it really been only three days since her sane, predictable, and, she admitted, utterly boring life had become so wickedly exciting?

With work, classes, and studying, Tess had allowed herself little time to socialize. As she watched Jack jog up the walk, she realized just how much she had missed spending time in the company of an intelligent, attractive man. A bizarre twist of fate had given her a fiancé, and even though the arrangement was fabricated and temporary, she intended to enjoy it. When another twinge of guilt assailed her, she told herself there were worse things in life than leading people to believe she planned to wed a handsome, smart young executive. As sins went, it hardly rated up there with murder or thievery. She had sacrificed and scrimped and put her own life on hold for the past several years; didn't that entitle her to this little bit of harmless excitement? She grabbed her coat and hurried out the door, meeting Jack on the front porch with a jaunty smile that camouflaged her jumping nerves and troubled conscience.

It took only fifteen minutes to drive from Tess's apartment to Betsy's modest ranch on Pleasant River's west side, but Tess made good use of the time, testing Jack on how well he recalled the details she had concocted for their fictional first meeting.

"Was the painting you admired by Manet or Monet?" he asked again.

"Monet. Claude Monet. Edouard Manet didn't do water lilies."

He nodded as the car pulled to a stop. "Well, it's now or never," he said, switching off the ignition. He jingled the keys in his hand, exposing his nerves. Tess refused to acknowledge her own jitters, even though she had chewed on her bottom lip until it felt raw and throbbing. She started to open the car door, but he stopped her with a hand on her arm.

"It's not too late to back out, you know. We could go in there and tell them the truth."

His offer was tempting, but her reasons for seeing this through hadn't changed. It was better to keep her family innocent. She just hoped they would forgive her if they ever learned the truth.

"Getting cold feet, Jack?" she asked. She kept her tone light, but her stomach was churning like a blender stuck on high.

"Cold feet? Heck, no." He sent her a wink, adding, "I'm saving those for June, sweetheart."

Tess's mother, sister Betsy, and brother-in-law Brian Hopper were lined up just inside the front door looking more like a firing squad than a welcoming committee. Jack resisted the urge to squirm under their scrutiny. None of them was smiling, although they did take turns politely shaking his hand while Tess made the introductions.

Tess's sister was the first to speak. Betsy was tall like Tess, with hair the same vibrant shade, but she wore it in a short, sleek bob. From behind wire-rimmed glasses she inspected Jack with a critical eye and remarked coolly, "I'd like to be able to say we've heard a lot about you, Jack, but we haven't. My sister has been incredibly tight-lipped about the man she is suddenly planning to marry."

"Betsy!" Tess admonished, sending Jack an apologetic smile. "I thought the point of my bringing him to Sunday supper was so you could get to know him, not stand there and insult him."

After her initial spurt of outrage Tess flushed guiltily, and Jack wondered if it had just occurred to her that Betsy had every right to question Tess's relationship with him. More right, in fact, than Betsy could possibly imagine.

"Tess, it's okay," he assured her. He took her hand and gave it a gentle squeeze, then kept it tucked inside his own damp palm in a gesture of support. He hated that he was the cause of so much friction in a family that, unlike his own, was very close. "The people who love you have every right to question me and my motives."

"I'm glad you feel that way," Brian said, taking a threatening step forward. "As I'm sure you understand, we feel rather protective of Tess."

The man appeared to be around Jack's age and about his height, but he was built like a linebacker. Tess had mentioned that Brian worked in construction, and it seemed clear that years of hefting steel beams and swinging a hammer had given him what other men joined gyms and popped anabolic steroids to achieve. Working outdoors for much of the year had caused fine lines to feather around his eyes, and twin grooves bracketed his mouth, evidence of easy laughter and a ready smile. But Jack noticed he wasn't smiling now. Brian was glaring at Jack with barely restrained violence simmering in his cool blue eyes.

"I wouldn't do anything to hurt Tess," Jack replied earnestly. "I can promise you all that."

Brian gave only a curt nod, appearing to reserve judgment.

"Do you love her?" Rita Donovan asked, drawing Jack's full attention. She stood almost a head shorter than her daughters did, but her steely gaze told him that despite her small stature she would be a formidable opponent. "That's all I need to know. Do you love my baby girl?"

Beside him, Jack felt Tess stiffen as she waited for him to respond. They had anticipated a lot of questions about their supposed love affair. But it had never occurred to either of them that anyone would dare to cut through all of the incidentals of their engagement and ask them point-blank if they loved one another.

He glanced at Tess, whose face had gone as white and rigid as marble, then back at her mother, who stood before him with her chin angled stubbornly, her gaze unwavering. The easiest answer, he knew, would be to say, "Yes, I love your daughter." But he couldn't force the words past his lips, even for the sake of preserving all the other lies they had told.

"Your daughter, Mrs. Donovan, is the most amazing woman I have ever met," he said at last. "She is kind and good and so beautiful she takes my breath away.'' The words came out with conviction, because, he realized, they were true. He raised Tess's hand to his lips and gently kissed the back of it. Looking at Tess, he admitted, ''I'm so lucky to have found her.''

After Jack's romantic declaration, everyone seemed to relax a little. Tess watched her mother nod, satisfied with his reply and seeming not to notice that he had never really answered her question. Brian grunted and slapped Jack's back in welcome, almost sending him sprawling on the floor. And Betsy returned to being the gracious hostess, leading them all into the small living room. As they took their seats, she offered them refreshments.

''Mom, Brian, why don't you keep Jack company while Tess and I get the coffee,'' she said. She didn't wait for a response, but snagged Tess by the arm and nearly dragged her from the room. The kitchen door had barely swung shut behind them when Betsy rounded on her. Gripping both of her arms, she said, ''Honey, I love you so much. You know there's nothing you can't tell me, right?''

''Of course, I know that,'' Tess replied. But with all the lies stretching between them, she found it impossible to maintain eye contact. Her observant sister apparently didn't miss that fact.

''Sweetie, you're not in trouble, are you?'' Betsy asked, her voice deadly calm and barely above a whisper.

Tess's mouth dropped open as realization dawned. ''Oh my God! You think I'm pregnant?''

Indignation came first. How could Betsy think Tess would surrender her innocence to a man she had just met? Then she remembered that Betsy assumed Tess had known Jack for several months; that she thought they were engaged to be married.

"It's okay," Betsy hastily assured her. "I wouldn't think less of you for, um, sleeping with Jack. I mean, Brian and I didn't wait till the wedding night to, um, consummate our relationship. There aren't many blushing brides these days. But if you're marrying this man because of, well, the result of a moment of passion…" she gestured vaguely, and Tess wondered just how many euphemisms her sister would use if allowed to go on. She decided to take pity on her.

"Betsy, I am *not* pregnant. Jack and I aren't really…" She wanted to say the words, but she couldn't force them past her lips. Tess turned her back on her sister, fiddling with the fringed edge of a dish towel that lay in a soggy heap next to the sink. "What I mean to say is that Jack and I haven't…I can promise you there's absolutely no way I am carrying Jack's baby."

"Well, okay," Betsy said, laying a hand on Tess's arm. "I figured that was the case, since you're not getting married until June, but I just wanted to know for sure that you're marrying him for all the right reasons."

Tess smiled, but said nothing. What could she say when she and Jack weren't even really engaged for all the right reasons?

To Tess's utter amazement, dinner was a pleasant experience. Jack Maris, she discovered, fitted right in with her family. He talked sports with her burly brother-in-law, insisting the Bruins had a chance at the Stanley Cup. He advised her mother on the benefits of mutual funds and Roth IRAs. He praised her sister's cooking, earning a beaming smile from Betsy, and complimented Rita on raising two lovely daughters. Throughout the meal, he charmed them all with his easy laughter and wry sense of humor. And Tess found herself dangerously close to believing that he really meant the heated looks he gave her from across the dinner table.

It was almost four o'clock when Jack pushed his chair back from the table and said, "That was delicious and I certainly enjoyed meeting all of you, but I'm afraid I have a plane to catch. I'd better take Tess home now or I'll miss my flight."

"We'd like to go with you to the airport," Betsy said, rising to clear away the dishes. From the look that passed between her and Brian it seemed obvious they had talked about this earlier. "If you don't mind, that is. We can bring Tess home afterward."

Tess caught Jack's uneasy look. His bags were packed and in the trunk of his car. He had planned to take her home after dinner and then head for the airport. It was what they had discussed and she didn't doubt that he was as eager as she was for the visit to end, especially while it was going so well.

"I don't mind," he said. "But it's really not necessary. I have a rental car that I have to return to the airport anyway."

"It's no trouble at all," Betsy assured him. "Besides, it will give you and Tess a little more time together before you have to say goodbye."

Pleasant River's small airport had only one terminal. Jack checked in at the gate and got his seat assignment, then returned to where Tess and her family sat in stiff, armless chairs.

"It appears my flight will be on time." He dropped into the chair next to Tess and stretched a proprietary arm over the back of her seat. Looking across at Betsy, he said, "That really was a terrific meal. Thanks again for having me."

"Oh, you're welcome. We'll do it again when you get back from Boston."

He hadn't realized his arm had moved from the back of the chair to Tess's shoulder, or that his fingers had begun to lightly caress her upper arm in slow even strokes, until he noticed Betsy's indulgent smile.

"Remember how we were when we were first dating, Brian?" she asked, laying a hand on her husband's knee. "You could turn me inside out with a smile or a simple touch, just like Jack here's doing to Tess."

His hand stilled, and he turned to look at Tess. She was blushing furiously and refused to meet his gaze.

"You two make a handsome couple," Betsy went on, either oblivious to her sister's embarrassment or taking a sibling's delight in prolonging it.

"Yes, they certainly do," Rita added, smiling warmly at Jack and Tess. "And I'm sure they will make beautiful babies together, just as you and Brian will once you get around to it."

The words were issued with a mother's gentle urging, and Jack saw Betsy roll her eyes. Apparently Rita made no bones about the fact that she wanted to be a grandmother. But, as he sat there with his arm wrapped around Tess it wasn't the thought of becoming a parent that had his insides quivering like jelly.

It was the process leading up to it. The embraces, the kisses, the nights of sweet passion.

He swallowed thickly, relieved when the boarding announcement for his flight came across the public address system.

"Well, that's me." He straightened, feeling suddenly torn about going.

He shook hands with Brian, but Betsy and Rita insisted on hugging him.

"You're as good as family, now," Rita explained, wrapping her thin arms around him. He had to stoop to fully return the embrace, and his conscience nudged him hard at deceiving what was clearly a very kind and generous woman.

That left just Tess. She stood back from the others, looking suddenly shy and nervous. The navy corduroy jumper and white turtleneck she wore made her look like a schoolgirl—young and a little prim. But the riot of flaming curls that framed her face and twisted down her back had Jack thinking of things that were decadent and very adult.

"Come here," he said, and she went willingly, almost eagerly into the circle of his arms.

She felt good there, he decided, soft in all the places a woman should be soft. Her hair teased his nose and smelled like apple blossoms, whetting different appetites. Into her ear he whispered, "Are you going to miss me?"

"More than I thought possible," she answered, sounding baffled but sincere.

He gave her smooth cheek a chaste peck and reluctantly released her. "I'll call you when I get in tonight."

He hadn't decided if he really meant the words or

if he'd said them for her family's benefit, but she nodded and forced a smile to her lips. He was stepping away from her when Betsy piped up.

"Jack, you're going to be gone for two weeks. Surely you can kiss your fiancée with a little more passion than that," she teased. Gray eyes so like Tess's shimmered with amusement.

He watched Tess's cheeks flame and despite his own embarrassment, he couldn't resist the temptation she posed. He had been wondering what those full lips would taste like since the first time he'd seen her waiting tables in Earl's Place.

"Tess, they want to see passion." He said it lightly, his gaze riveted on her lips. With a little tug, he pulled her solidly against him, surprising a little "oh" out of her.

"Two weeks is an awfully long time." Enfolded in Jack's arms, Tess didn't hear him whisper the words as much as she felt them flutter against her face. He held her gaze as his head descended and their lips met. Her eyes drifted shut. The kiss began slow and tentative, erotic for all its chaste simplicity. But then his tongue slid along the seam of her lips in question, and Tess answered—greedily, hungrily and utterly without reservation. She nearly forgot about her mother, sister and brother-in-law, who stood not five feet away shuffling their feet, probably a little uncomfortable watching the wanton display before them. And she did forgot about all the lies she and Jack had told. Indeed, the line between truth and illusion blurred into oblivion while she drowned in the taste and texture of his kiss.

She was dazed and a little dizzy when it ended. Never before had a kiss caused the world to tilt on its axis quite the way this one had. Then she realized it was not the world that had tilted; she had. Jack had bent her over his arm until her back was nearly parallel to the floor. His face hovered just inches above hers, and he smiled rakishly while her family stared, murmuring about Jack's very dramatic and romantic farewell.

"Is that enough passion for you?" he called to Betsy as he restored Tess to her feet. Her sister giggled and flashed him a thumbs-up sign.

Foolishness made Tess's fast-beating heart stutter almost painfully in her chest. Of course the kiss hadn't really meant anything. Like everything else between them, it was calculated to deceive. But Tess's family hadn't been the only ones fooled this time. She pasted a smile on her face and waved to him as he walked away, blinking furiously as her eyes watered and stung. His hands were full with a briefcase, newspaper and small carry-on bag, but he nodded to them all, saving a wink for Tess just before he disappeared through the door where a flight attendant stood taking tickets. Tess held off the tears until his plane had taxied down the runway.

"Hey," Betsy soothed, giving her shoulders a gentle squeeze. "Let's have none of that now. He'll be back before you know it. And if that kiss was any indication, he'll be eager to make up for lost time."

Tess touched trembling fingers to her lips. Yes, she thought miserably, he would be coming back to Pleasant River in just two weeks. But he would be coming back for a job at Faust Enterprises; he wouldn't be coming back for Tess Donovan.

The day after returning to Boston, Jack sent Tess roses, a dozen long-stemmed beauties the same shade as her lush lips. But the card he included contained nothing but an impersonal "thank you." This was business, he told himself, even if he did thoroughly appreciate the very personal sacrifices she had made for him. Still, he didn't call her, even though he'd told her he would. He thought about it. He even picked up the telephone half a dozen times, only to stop himself before dialing her number. It was that kiss, he decided. It had his mind going places it had no business going.

Like the dream he'd had the second night back. In it he and Tess again stood in the airport, kissing good-bye, but this time it didn't end quite the same way as before. With their mouths still fused in passion, he unfastened her jumper, sending navy corduroy pooling around her feet. Under the dress she wore not a prim white turtleneck, but a sexy black teddy. Red garters held up sheer black hose, and on her feet were three-inch-high stiletto heels. He ran a reverent hand from her narrow waist to the underside of one full breast. He was slipping that hand inside the lacy top of her teddy when his alarm clock went off. Blasted thing. He'd awoken fully aroused and had been irritable ever since. And he decided he had to contact her, but he didn't want to do it by telephone. He worried he would say something foolish like, "I miss you." Or ask something lecherous like, "What are you wearing?"

It wasn't possible, he reminded himself, to go from being "engaged" to just dating. Not when Cora Faust's loose lips undoubtedly would ensure that the entire town of Pleasant River expected Jack and Tess to marry, and by the end of June no less. Between now and then, they had to stage a huge and very public fight if they wanted their breakup to be convincing. They couldn't do that and go to the movies, too.

Besides, Jack told himself, inevitably Tess would want more from him than he could give. He'd glimpsed her family life. She apparently came from a long line of happily monogamous people who not only exchanged vows, they truly believed in the institution of marriage. Unfortunately for him, long-term commitments just weren't in the Maris genes, as his father's five wives, mother's four husbands, and sister's recent divorce proved rather painfully. Nancy had pointed that out to him the night she walked out.

Nancy. They had been together for six comfortable and companionable years, but, as she had so acerbically noted before leaving, if all he wanted was comfort and companionship, he should get a dog. She wanted permanency. She wanted a legally binding commitment. She wanted a wedding ring. The way the thought of it all made his throat constrict, she might as well have put a noose around his neck.

Jack had been quite content to continue their arrangement: dating exclusively, but with all the exit doors clearly marked. Funny thing was, even after spending six years with her, now that she was engaged to another he didn't really miss her. He missed waking up next to a warm and willing woman. He missed the company and shared interests, and coming home to an apartment where music was playing and the scents of supper greeted him. But he couldn't remember ever kissing Nancy and feeling like he had after kissing Tess: reckless, breathless, and more than a little confused. Lust, he decided. It had to be lust.

Jack riffled through boxes that already had been

taped shut until he found a pen and some stationery. Then, for the first time in years, he sat down and wrote a woman a letter, telling himself he wasn't doing it because of the comment Tess had made to Cora Faust about getting to know a man by the way he put his thoughts on paper.

He started the letter five times, stumbling over the greeting, until he finally settled on the appropriate if uninspired, Dear Tess. Then the words just seemed to flow.

Three decades worth of junk have been packed up in cardboard boxes, waiting for the movers to arrive. Funny how you accumulate stuff over the years without even realizing it, then you go to move and it takes a U-Haul to accommodate it all. I still remember moving to my first apartment. I only needed the trunk of my car to hold all my possessions. Of course, back then I slept in a sleeping bag rather than on a queen-sized cherry four-poster bed, and my living-room furniture consisted of milk crates and a futon.

It seems strange to be moving to a small town. I've always thought of myself as an urban dweller, and I've enjoyed Boston's rich history and cultural amenities, but I don't think I'll really miss this city. I'd say it's never really felt like home, but then, no place has.

Speaking of home, I thought I had better tell you about my prospects for a house just in case someone asks you. As my fiancée you would be expected to know the details.

Maybe you're familiar with the Cape Cod

over on Ashbury? My friend Davis Marx and I went by it the day after we had dinner at the Saint Sebastian. It needs a little work inside—it still has gold shag carpeting and red velvet wallpaper—but it has three good-sized bedrooms and a den with built-in bookcases. I have lots of books, including a collection of rather rare first editions, so bookcases are a must. The yard is fenced and big enough for a dog to run, not that I have a dog. My life is too busy for pets right now, but maybe someday. Your fiancé, Tess, is a dog lover. Hope you don't own a cat.

Davis and I also toured a ranch over on Hemingway. It's got a walkout basement and gourmet kitchen, but the master bedroom isn't very large, and the windows are small. No big bay with a window seat in the living room, either.

He almost added, I don't think you would like it as well. He mentally shook himself and continued.

I'm leaning toward the Cape Cod.

I should be back the Sunday before Thanksgiving. I'm driving my car straight through from Boston, so I'm not sure how long it will take. I'll be staying at the Saint Sebastian until I close on a house. Call me if you need anything, otherwise I'll be in touch. And thanks again. It's a pleasure being engaged to you.

Jack sat for a few minutes worrying over how to end the letter. Finally, he simply scratched his name across the bottom of the page and hastily stuffed it into the envelope.

* * *

Tess saw the Boston return address and ripped open the letter as she stood on the landing. She read it twice, her heart thudding almost painfully in her chest as she sifted through the words looking for clues as to how he really felt about her. If they were there, she couldn't decipher them.

She returned to her apartment, intending to study, but she found herself reading Jack's letter for a third time. Idly, she traced the tip of her index finger over the masculine cursive, trying to imagine where he had been when he'd written it and what he had been thinking. He had nice handwriting, she thought, bold and confident. It suited him, and for no reason she could fathom, just staring at those pen strokes made her miss him all the more.

"This is ridiculous," she said aloud, putting the letter aside. "I have studying to do."

She opened her notebook to a blank page, intending to take down the pertinent information from the chapter her political science professor had assigned in class. But the words *Dear Jack*, were the first she penned.

I received your letter just this morning. I was surprised to hear from you, but pleasantly so.

Does this mean you're thinking about me, too? she wondered, but wrote,

The house on Ashbury sounds delightful, a real find. I can tell you that the neighborhood is simply wonderful. Mature trees and large, well-tended yards. I hope you don't mind raking leaves, because you'll have plenty of them.

I have a confession to make. I'm playing hooky. I should be studying right now, but writing to you seemed like more fun than reading about the impeachment powers of Congress. Only twelve more credits after this semester and I'll have my degree. That's what I tell myself when I get discouraged, but sometimes it seems like it might as well be twelve hundred.

But enough of my complaining. So, you're a dog person? I can't tell you how relieved I am. I would have had to break off our "engagement" if you'd been into cats. They're too sneaky and indifferent for my taste. I prefer the utter adoration of a hound. Who else will greet you so enthusiastically when you arrive home after a long day?

Would you? she allowed herself to wonder. Still thinking that thought, she scratched, Miss you, and signed her name along the bottom of the page.

Tess smiled as she folded the letter and sealed it in an envelope. Humming, she copied his return address onto the outside and affixed a stamp. Then, to ensure she could not change her mind about mailing it, she pulled on a coat, walked to the corner mailbox, and dropped it inside.

Jack hadn't expected a reply to his letter, but when he saw the return address he tossed aside the bills and assorted solicitations the mailman had delivered and ripped into it with the enthusiasm of a child opening a gift. He couldn't recall the last time anyone, let alone a woman, had sent him an actual letter. His mother or father occasionally remembered to send a birthday card and his sister sometimes e-mailed him at Christmas. But a letter? He smiled as he read what Tess had written, oddly touched that she had taken the time to reply when he would see her within the week. Then, for no reason he could fathom, he carefully folded the note and tucked it into his billfold.

Chapter Four

Tess stifled a yawn and continued to plunk away at the keys of the electric typewriter that sat humming on her kitchen table. The thing was ancient and more than a little temperamental, but she couldn't afford a computer and the public library had closed more than two hours ago. As usual, she had waited until the last minute; the research paper for her political science class was due the next day. The doorbell pealed just as she finished typing a sentence, causing her to add a couple of extra characters.

She muttered a mild oath, then glanced at the clock. Irritation turned to confusion. It was late and she wasn't expecting anyone. The doorbell sounded a second time as she pulled a cardigan over her faded T-shirt and sweatpants and hurried down the stairs to the front door.

Through the large oval of glass in the center of the door, Tess spied Jack. His hands were tucked into his pockets and the collar of his leather bomber jacket was turned up against the cold. Thanksgiving was only days away, but the temperatures were reading more like January.

"Jack!" She flicked open the locks, trying to tamp down on her excitement in the process. It wouldn't do to greet him like some adoring teenager suffering her first crush.

"This is a surprise," she said, holding her grin in check as she held open the door for him. He stepped inside, bringing a gust of chilly air with him. Tess pulled the cardigan tighter around her, but not before she saw Jack's gaze stray downward. From his guilty expression, she knew he'd noticed that she wasn't wearing a bra under the T-shirt.

"I hope I'm not disturbing you. I just got back into town, but I was too keyed up to sleep. I drank a little too much caffeine while on the road," he admitted. "I was driving around and saw your light. I hope you don't mind my just dropping in?"

"No, of course not. I was just working on a research paper." She blew out a frustrated breath. "It seems like I'm *always* working on a research paper or studying for some exam. I feel like a professional student."

He gave her arm a squeeze. "Graduation day will be here before you know it. So, do you have time for a break?"

"Sure," she lied. "The paper will keep."

"I, uh, have something for you. I thought about mailing it, but I was worried the post office might lose it."

She couldn't stop the grin that spread across her face. "You have something for me?" she repeated.

"Why don't we go up to your apartment, little girl,

and I'll show you what it is?'' he teased, eliciting a laugh when he raised his eyebrows Groucho Marx-style.

Her apartment was barely half the size of the one Jack had shared with Nancy in Boston, but if he'd had to describe it in a word he would have said *homey*. Lace curtains hung at the windows and a collection of colorful throw pillows lined the back of a lumpy couch. Tastefully framed watercolors adorned the wall, and a candy dish full of peppermints and a crystal bowl full of potpourri sat on one small end table. He caught a whiff of the faint floral scent he had come to associate with Tess and smiled. Her tiny living room invited guests inside, all but begging them to slough off their coats and their troubles, and prop their weary feet atop the armchair's well-worn ottoman. The place was warm and welcoming in a way that the glass, chrome and leather he and Nancy had decorated their Boston apartment with had never been.

"Nice place you have here."

Tess waited anxiously while Jack hung his jacket on the brass coat tree that stood next to the door and pulled something from its pocket.

Cocking up an eyebrow, he said, "It dawned on me after I returned to Boston that we never actually solved the dilemma of the absent engagement ring."

His tone was serious, but humor danced in his eyes.

"Nope. I'm still ringless," she replied lightheartedly. She wagged her left hand in front of his face for inspection, and with a comical sigh of resignation confided, "People around here just assume I'm marrying a cheapskate."

"Not for long." With an exaggerated flourish, he

opened his hand. On the palm sat a small square box that looked rather old. The black leather that covered it was worn at the edges and the small metal clasp that held it together was a tarnished brown.

Tess's breath hitched in her throat and the teasing humor evaporated, leaving her acutely aware that her hand shook when she reached out to take the box from him. Silently cursing her foolishness, she reminded herself that it didn't mean anything; it was just another prop. But when she opened the box, her eyes misted anyway. The ring was absolutely beautiful.

"Oh, Jack." She didn't know what she had expected him to give her to make the illusion of their engagement complete, but this wasn't it. The marquis-cut diamond was at least a carat, surrounded by smaller stones and set in ornate white gold filigree.

"It was my grandmother's," he said. He looked as surprised by his wistful tone as she was.

"It's a family heirloom? Are you sure you trust me with it? I mean, I'd be just as satisfied with something that came out of a Cracker Jack box, for heaven's sake."

She said it, and she meant it, but her fingers itched to touch the ring. It was exactly the kind of engagement ring she'd dreamed of someday wearing.

"I trust you," he said solemnly, his voice sounding almost like a vow. Carefully, he extracted the ring from the box. The diamond caught the light, its radiance dazzling her. She sucked in a ragged breath, and wished the moment could be as real as the gem winking back at her. He reached for her left hand, surprising a nervous giggle out of her.

"I can put it on myself," she objected, but she

didn't try to tug away her hand when he continued to slide the ring onto her fourth finger. Mesmerized, she could only stare as he turned her hand and the heavy stone shifted slightly. The band's fit was a little loose, but it would do.

"There was no need for you to do that," she whispered. "There's no one here to fool."

"No," he agreed, his voice hoarse and low. But he didn't release her hand. Instead, he raised it to his lips, brushing her knuckles with the barest hint of a kiss. Tess felt his breath, hot and uneven, flutter across the back of her hand. It raised goosebumps on her flesh even as it made her burn. Her eyes drifted shut. She bit back a moan as unfamiliar pleasure shimmied up her spine. What was he doing to her?

Whatever it was, Jack wasn't through. Slowly, he reeled her in until barely an inch separated their bodies. Confused, Tess opened her eyes, but there were no answers to be found in Jack's gaze. He looked as perplexed as she—perplexed, but not about to retreat. With his free hand, he caressed the slope of her neck before burying his fingers in her hair.

"I love this," he breathed. One side of his mouth crooked up as he broke eye contact briefly to skim his gaze over the curls rioting around her face. She'd always considered her hair too red and wild to be pretty, but Jack's possessive smile told her he felt differently. The pad of his thumb stroked her cheek, and then he lifted her chin just a fraction. She watched his brow furrow as if he were trying to puzzle out some equation. As his head lowered toward hers, he seemed to reach a conclusion.

"God, I want you," she thought she heard him murmur.

The kiss in the airport hadn't prepared Tess for this. Jack's mouth moved over hers—thorough, possessive and just a little rough with need. It snatched away her breath, making the blood heat in her veins and then pool in places that left her feeling weighted and full. It seemed her only choice was to respond. Instinct had Tess twining her arms around Jack's neck and urging him closer until even the well-worn cotton of her T-shirt seemed too great a barrier.

Unprecedented need—frightening, thrilling—swept through her with all the subtlety of a California brush fire. As a unit, they backed up a step at a time until Tess felt the couch brush the backs of her legs. Jack lowered her to the cushions without breaking off the kiss, and then she was beneath him, his full weight pressing against her until she felt his desire most intimately. While he trailed hot kisses over her cheek and nibbled on her earlobe, experienced hands inched up her torso beneath her shirt and lean hips rotated against hers in an age-old rhythm. Tess might be a virgin, but she knew what would come next. And it scared the heck out of her, because for just a moment, she considered agreeing.

Sanity returned in a rush, shame quick on its heels. How foolish, she berated herself. Take away the bogus engagement and the beautiful ring and it would be just sex. Casual sex with someone who liked her and obviously was attracted to her, but who had made her no promises save one: Their phony engagement would end once it had served his purpose. Not exactly a promise to surrender one's virtue to, Tess reminded herself ruthlessly. As it was, she feared he already had her heart.

She pushed against Jack's shoulders until he was

forced to stop his erotic exploration of her neck and look at her.

"I—I think you should go," she whispered.

"Go?" he repeated blankly, studying her as if she spoke a foreign language. And perhaps she did. A man as good-looking and sexy as Jack probably didn't get turned down often, especially at this late stage of the seduction. From some unknown reserve, she dredged up the strength to be firm.

"I think this would be a mistake."

"Mistake?" Again, he echoed her words, although this time his eyes lost their glazed appearance.

Tess gave a jerky nod, not trusting her voice enough to speak while he studied her so intently. Under his gaze, she felt her face color, the heat of a moment before seeming to collect in her cheeks.

Expelling a ragged breath, Jack slowly extricated himself from her limbs until they were both safely seated on the couch, half a cushion separating their bodies. Tess tugged down her T-shirt and pulled the cardigan together, while Jack scrubbed a hand over his face and mumbled something incoherent.

As his breathing evened out and the blood winging through his veins slowed and cooled, Jack had time to regret his actions. He shouldn't have come. Not with all this need raging inside him, snapping his control, and making him behave so recklessly. He had suspected it before, but he should have known it for a fact. Tess wasn't a woman who would eagerly consent to some brief, albeit mutually satisfying, fling.

He turned, planning to toss off some witty quip to lighten the moment, but the sad, uncertain smile wavering on her lips stopped him. My God, what had he done? With an oath directed at himself, he stalked to the door, yanked his jacket off the coat tree and banged down the steps without saying goodbye.

Tess awoke the next morning feeling sluggish and irritable after only a couple of hours of fitful sleep. She had dreamed of Jack, she was sure, but only wispy images of the dreams remained, teasing her memory and making her yearn for things she knew she had no right to want.

She hurried through her morning routine, securing her hair in a tight braid and donning her walking clothes. She stuffed a sweater and a pair of faded jeans into a tote bag and grabbed her research paper. It would hardly earn her an A, she thought, as she stowed it in her backpack with her textbooks, but at least she had managed to finish it after Jack left. That had been no simple task, since all coherent thought seemed to have vanished into the chilly night with him.

She glanced at her watch as she loped down the stairs and hurried to her car. Maybe she would have time to walk four miles this morning if she kept her pace brisk and battering. She preferred physical exhaustion to this emotional fatigue.

Twenty-five minutes later, the first mile had put a painful stitch in her side and her lungs were burning from the cold air, but Tess did her best to ignore both, lengthening her stride as if trying to outpace her problems. The most pressing one, however, insisted on catching up.

"Tess, wait!" a familiar male voice hollered.

Her traitorous heart thrilled as it always did at the sound of his voice saying her name, but she was tempted to keep going, to pretend she hadn't heard

Jack. That would be juvenile, she decided. So she armed herself with indifference, and turned around with a bland smile quirking up the corners of her mouth.

"Good morning," she called. Her breath created a misty haze in the frigid morning light. Jack drew up alongside her, huffing as if he had just completed the Boston Marathon.

"I thought I might see you out here," he said, once he caught his breath. "I wanted to apologize for last night."

His gaze searched her face, lingering on her puffy eyes and perhaps taking note of the dark smudges beneath them. It mortified her to think he would see the evidence that she had cried herself to sleep, so she pulled off her gloves and bent down, pretending to tighten her shoelaces. The diamond on her finger caught her eye. It seemed obscene to be wearing it, but she couldn't bring herself to take it off. She had even slept with it on, the unfamiliar weight of it somehow feeling right on her left ring finger.

"There's no need to apologize, really," she assured him without looking up.

"Maybe," he allowed. "But I am sorry. Here you are, doing me a huge favor, and I try to...I had no right, Tess."

She tightened the laces until she feared she might have cut off the circulation to her feet, but she still couldn't bring herself to look at him. So she straightened and made a show of pulling on her gloves.

"Forgive me?" he asked.

"There's really nothing to forgive," she said at last, amazed that she could speak around the wad of misery clogging her throat. His behavior may have disappointed her, but if her heart was a little bruised, well, it was no one's fault but her own. So he hadn't offered her a relationship beyond the physical; he'd said he found her attractive. People went to bed together all the time for reasons even less substantial than mutual attraction.

"I'm glad you feel that way. I wasn't sure. I mean, I came on a little strong, um, stepped over some pretty clear boundaries. But you're a tempting woman. A man would have to be dead not to want you. Still, I..." He seemed to struggle for the right words, and then he took her hand and gave it a gentle squeeze, forcing her to look at him. "I like you, Tess. And I want us to be friends. I hope my behavior last night won't do anything to prevent that."

It took all of Tess's willpower not to scream. *Friends?* He wanted to be friends? No doubt if they had slept together he would still be proposing the same benign relationship.

"Look, Jack, you made a pass at me. I think I'll get over it," she said, spearing him with an impatient look. She hoped she sounded sophisticated and maybe just a little bit bored, as if gorgeous men kissed her until she was horizontal every day.

"You wound me," he teased, but he looked away from her, gazing at some distant point on the horizon.

She consulted her watch. "I don't mean to be rude, but I've got to go or I'll be late for work."

"Of course. Tess, I..." The rest of his words disappeared with his frozen breath. After an awkward moment, he finally said, "What time do you get off work today?"

"Five, but I have class from six till nine," she told him.

More awkward silence followed, then he blurted out, "I'm buying the house on Ashbury. The one I wrote to you about."

She smiled, genuinely happy for him. "That's great."

"I don't suppose you'd like to come over and see it? I don't close on it till next week, but it's empty and the real estate agent is a friend of Ira Faust's, so she was nice enough to give me a key." He plunged his hands into the pockets of his sweatpants, looking almost boyish. "I could order a pizza and pick you up after your class."

"Jack..." the single syllable felt as if it were dragged from deep inside her.

"I promise to be on my best behavior." He pulled his hands from his pockets and held them up in supplication, giving her a grin that creased his stubbled cheeks. "My fiancée really should see the house where we're going to live once we're married." Then he shook his head and in a sober voice added, "I...I really want you to see it, Tess."

She couldn't resist the lonely appeal in his voice. What could it hurt? she decided. She could pretend last night hadn't happened if he could. And she was curious about the house. No, that wasn't quite accurate. She was curious about where Jack would be living. She wanted to be able to picture him sitting in his kitchen or looking out his living-room window. For some reason, that seemed extremely important at this moment.

"I like pepperoni and mushrooms," she told him. "And lots of cheese."

Tess noticed the windows first. Although it was dark outside, she knew that during the day, when the thick draperies were peeled back, sunlight would flood the living room, its golden warmth spilling cheerfully into every corner. Plants would thrive here. *She* would thrive here. She shook off that foolish thought, but she couldn't hide her enthusiasm.

"I love it!" She spun around in a giddy circle. "It's absolutely perfect."

"Yeah." He looked around, as if seeing it through her eyes. "I think so, too." Satisfaction shone on his face, and he seemed to be surprised to find it suited him so well.

"It's got a great den. Come on." He grabbed her by the hand and pulled her down a long hallway, leaving the pizza box on the living-room floor next to their discarded jackets.

"Just look at this woodwork," he said, awe evident in his tone as he stroked the mantel on the den's fireplace. His touch was reminiscent of a lover's caress. "Look at the craftsmanship. The new houses today, they don't have this kind of detail."

"That's one of the things I like about my apartment," Tess confessed. "That place is old as dirt and the plumbing gives me fits, but I do love the oak floors and wainscoting."

He nodded in agreement. "I debated living in one of those apartments over on Rayburn until I could build a home of my own. And the Fausts suggested that new subdivision that's going in off the interstate. There are some prime lots for sale at reasonable prices. But this place has everything I could ask for and so much...I don't know. I guess, personality."

As Jack said it, he marveled that he felt that way. He thought about Nancy and her penchant for the modern. A penchant he'd long thought he shared. But those angular structures now struck him as hopelessly garish with their lack of gables, ivy trellises and cobblestone garden paths. Nancy would find this house quaint, he knew, but uninhabitable. It did not have walk-in closets or large bathrooms with jet tubs. It did not have intercoms or a state-of-the-art sound system wired throughout its rooms. It didn't even have an attached garage with a remote door opener.

"It feels like home," he said quietly. "I really like it." Tess turned to look at him, her expression one of understanding.

She smiled and gave his arm a gentle squeeze. "I'm happy for you."

Jack held her gaze for another moment, and then he glanced down at the delicate hand still pressing his arm. The gem on her finger caught his eye, and his thoughts strayed almost involuntarily to the fact that the rest of Pleasant River thought they soon would be living here together as husband and wife. The master bedroom was just down the hall. Empty now, but Jack could picture his in there. And he needed only a little help from his imagination to conjure up the image of Tess sprawled across its satin sheets, wrapped in nothing but her glorious hair.

Swallowing a moan, he summoned up every ounce of willpower and hitched a thumb over his shoulder in the direction of the living room. "Pizza?" he croaked.

"Sure. I'm famished."

Jack spread their coats on the drafty floor while Tess opened two cans of cola. With their backs resting flush against the wall and the pizza box sandwiched between their hips, they dug in hungrily. Around them, the house groaned and creaked, but the sounds were comforting instead of eerie. As they ate their fill, the conversation dwindled, leaving in its wake a silence that was companionable rather than awkward. Still, Tess began to feel uneasy. Just sitting next to Jack had her questioning the decision she'd made the night before. Wise or not, her body's re-action to his nearness was virtually impossible to ig-nore.

It was all Jack's fault, of course. Out of the corner of her eye, she studied him. Why did the man have to be so temptingly gorgeous? A day's worth of stub-ble shadowed his jaw, and his hair was slightly di-sheveled. If possible, these minor imperfections only made him more attractive.

He pivoted to pull the last slice of pizza from the box and caught her looking at him. His hands stilled, and the easy smile on his lips flattened into a serious line as awareness sharpened his expression.

"Don't look at me like that, Tess," he warned softly. "Or I'll wind up owing you another apology."

She dropped her gaze and fidgeted with the napkin in her lap. "I haven't changed my mind," she said, voicing the thought more for her own clarification than for his.

"I know, just wishful thinking on my part," he said, sounding bemused. He tossed the untouched pizza slice back into the box. "What do you say we change the subject, huh?"

"I'd appreciate the favor."

"Ah, speaking of favors, I have another one to ask of you."

"Another one?" She rolled her eyes, feigning exasperation, relieved to let humor supplant sexual tension.

"'Fraid so. The Fausts are having a big to-do at their house on Thanksgiving. I guess since they don't have a family of their own they do it every year. I tried to get out of it by telling them we were going to your sister's house for dinner, but they're insisting we stop by later for cocktails. I can make up another excuse if you don't want to go with me."

Another evening spent with Jack. It must have been the masochist in her who responded, "That's all right. I'll go."

"Really? Hey, thanks. I'll pick you up around seven, if that's okay?" When she nodded, he asked, "Should I come by your apartment or will you still be with your family?"

"I'll be at Betsy's house," she said. Then a thought occurred to her. "Where are you having dinner, Jack?"

He lifted his shoulders. "I thought I'd pick up some Chinese and eat in my room at the Saint Sebastian." Her expression must have reflected how appalled she felt at the idea of him eating alone, because he added, "Don't feel sorry for me, Tess. I'm not really that big on the holidays."

Still, Tess didn't approve. Thanksgiving was about family and friends, home cooking and overeating. No one should spend it alone in some impersonal hotel room, eating stir-fry instead of the traditional turkey, stuffing and cranberry sauce.

"That's silly. My sister makes enough food to feed a small army. You're welcome to come." Her motive for asking him to supper was purely humanitarian, she assured herself.

"I wasn't angling for an invitation." He wadded up his napkin and tossed it into the pizza box.

"I know, but I'm extending one. To my fiancé. Bets and Mom are expecting you to be there," she lied. She had told them just the day before that Jack had not yet returned from Boston.

"Well, in that case, I guess I'd better come."

Chapter Five

Tess primped. She told herself that wasn't what she was doing as she soaked in the bathtub and spent an extra fifteen minutes arranging her hair in a sleek French braid. She dabbed some perfume behind her ears and on her wrists and debated which shade of lipstick to wear, the nearly nude gloss she usually wore or the come-hither red Betsy had talked her into buying. All the while she convinced herself that spending a day with Jack had absolutely no bearing on her behavior.

As she secured the backings on her earrings, she heard the doorbell peal. Grabbing her long wool coat, she hurried down the steps, nearly twisting her ankle in the high heels she wore. She liked the fact that even when she was wearing heels, Jack still had a couple of inches on her. At five feet nine, Tess had worn her share of flats on dates. She opened the door and Jack stepped inside, freshly shaved and smelling of a spicy men's cologne. She could see the knot of his tie underneath the camel-colored overcoat he wore. He looked every inch the respected, prosperous young executive. And she wanted to look her part, too.

"I hope what I'm wearing is appropriate. You said the Fausts' party would be dressy."

She did a slow pirouette and had the satisfaction of hearing him swallow. Betsy had been kind enough to loan her the dress. The simple sheath of stretchy emerald material hugged Tess's body like a second skin.

"You look gorgeous," he said, helping her into her coat.

Her heart tripped around in her chest. Smiling over her shoulder at him, she said, "Shall we?"

If her family noticed the furtive glances that passed between Tess and Jack throughout dinner, they were kind enough not to comment on them. Or, Tess decided, maybe they were just too preoccupied with pumping the couple for wedding details.

"You haven't asked me to be your matron of honor yet, but I saw the most gorgeous dress at Chapel Bridal over in Piedmont." Betsy smiled warmly and helped herself to more turkey.

Tess noticed they were using the china Betsy and Brian had received as a wedding gift, and naturally her older sister had already asked Tess if she and Jack had picked out a china pattern, silverware, and crystal. That in turn had prompted a lengthy discussion on where the couple should register for gifts. Betsy and Rita suggested a department store in the next town, which Tess promised to consider in the hope the subject of her wedding would be closed. Apparently that hope was futile.

"So, what were you doing in Piedmont?" Tess asked.

Betsy shifted slightly in her seat and made a show of trickling a little gravy over her meat. Across the table her mother began to fiddle with her napkin.

"Oh, well, Mama and I thought we'd just go take a look at some dresses."

When Tess's mouth fell open, Betsy added with a guilty little chuckle, "We didn't buy anything yet. We just wanted to see what the wedding fashions are these days. June's not that far off, Tess, and these things take time. There are fittings and alterations." She cast an embarrassed glance Jack's way. "And, um, payment schedules. Those dresses aren't exactly cheap."

Jack looked as if he wanted to disappear. Tess caught his guilty look. No doubt he felt as horrible as she did. Her family was planning a wedding that would never take place, and they were already starting to save up their hard-earned dollars to pay for it.

"You're not mad, are you, dear?" Rita asked when Tess just sat there staring at the puddle of gravy in her mashed potatoes.

Mad? She was disgusted with herself, guilt-stricken about the deception she'd agreed to perpetuate, but how could she possibly be mad at them?

"N-no, Mom, I'm not mad." As a form of torture, she made herself ask, "So, did you find anything?"

Rita excitedly confessed, "I did find a nice dress. It's apricot-colored with a full skirt and a jewel-buttoned jacket." At fifty-eight, Tess's mother had enough feminine vanity to add, "Betsy says it makes me look ten years younger."

"Well, then you'll look more like a bridesmaid than the mother of the bride," Jack told her. Rita fluttered a hand in his direction, and Tess watched her mother flush with delight.

"Tess, you don't have class tomorrow night. Maybe you could ask Earl to let you off early and you, me, and Mom could drive over to Piedmont and try on dresses," Betsy said.

"Oh, that would be so much fun!" Rita cried, clapping her hands together enthusiastically.

Even Brian seemed to get caught up in the excitement as Jack and Tess sat there, eyes unblinking as yet another deception was piled onto the thin shoulders of all the others.

"You ladies can shop and then have dinner at that new rib place that opened just off the interstate."

"Oh, yes! Tess, what do you say?" Betsy pressed.

What could she say with three expectant faces turned in her direction? She glanced at Jack for help, but he looked as if he were choking on a bone.

"Uh, I guess. Earl owes me a favor for staying late a couple times last week. I think I can get him to let me off around three if one of the other waitresses can cover for me."

"Hey, while you girls are in Piedmont, Jack and I can go up to Skip's Pub, grab a couple of burgers and a pitcher of beer, and watch the hockey game on the big-screen TV. Wings are playing the Avalanche. How 'bout it, Jack?"

Jack gave Tess a helpless look, and seemed to shrug his shoulders in defeat. "I'll buy the first round."

Just as the women began to clear the table, Brian pushed back his chair and announced, "Well, it's time for football."

Tess had noticed that after almost seven years of marriage to her sister, Brian had developed a finely honed skill for making himself scarce whenever kitchen duty called.

"Lions are playing the Bears at the Silverdome," he told Jack. He stood up and stretched lazily before sauntering out of the room.

Jack flashed a smug male grin at Tess. "I guess I'd better go keep your brother-in-law company."

"You do that," she said dryly as she stacked dirty plates.

Jack and Brian were sitting on the couch shouting about a flag on the play when Tess entered the living room carrying two plates of pumpkin pie.

"What does the ref mean, *holding?*" Jack hollered at the television. "That wasn't holding!"

Tess rolled her eyes and held out a plate to him.

"The guy needs glasses," Brian agreed as he relieved her of the other plate of pie.

She was about to return to the kitchen when Jack scooted over on the couch and motioned with his fork for her to sit down. She hesitated only for an instant, then squeezed in between the two men. Her mother was washing; Betsy was drying. It didn't take three women to do dishes, she decided, feeling only a tiny bit guilty for abandoning them.

"Tess here knows a lot about football," Brian confided to Jack around a mouthful of pie.

"Really? And why is that?"

She barely heard the question. The feel of Jack's

lean hip pressed against hers on the couch was much too distracting. Delicious heat curled through her, radiating out from the point of contact. Brian, however, was big brother enough to help her through the awkward moments in life.

"Tess, honey, quit thinking about sex and answer the man." He leaned across her to smile at Jack. "You've sure got this girl's hormones all in a knot."

Tess wanted to wither between the couch cushions and take up residency with any spare change lurking there. But, of course, Brian wouldn't let her.

"Isn't she cute when she blushes, Jack? Say the S-word around Tess and she starts to look as if she's spent a couple of hours too many in the sun."

Jack coughed. She thought he might be trying to cover a laugh, but when she peered at him, he looked as tense as she felt.

"So, uh, why do you know so much about the game?" he asked in a voice just this side of tight.

"Game? Oh, yeah, football. I cover the high-school team for the *Pleasant River Beacon.* The season just ended." When Jack's eyebrows notched up, she added meaningfully, "They almost went to the state championships, but you knew that, *dear.*"

"Of course, I knew that, but refresh my memory. How did you get the job?"

"It started out as an internship of sorts a couple of years ago, but now I do it every fall. I'm hoping to work at the *Beacon* full-time after I graduate next semester, although I'm more interested in covering city hall or county government than high-school athletics. One of the reporters will be leaving after the first of the year. I've already put in my application.

I'm hoping they'll hire me even though I won't have my degree officially until May."

"They'd be fools not to snap you up," Jack declared. And he meant it. The woman worked full-time at Earl's, took a full load of college credits *and* managed to write for the local newspaper. She was simply amazing. Then, with a bemused shake of his head he murmured, "Football. No offense, but that seems an odd assignment for you."

"None taken." She smiled. "I'll admit that first season I didn't know the difference between a touchdown and a field goal, much less a two-point conversion. I think Mr. Applebee—he's the editor—only gave me the assignment because he figured I'd fail at it."

"So why doesn't this Applebee character like you?"

Jack watched Tess fidget with an earring. "It's not that he dislikes me," she hedged.

"Oh, he dislikes her," Brian supplied happily. "Tess dated his son in high school. Craig wanted to marry her, but she wanted to go to college. Mr. Applebee is still bent out of shape. But I think he'll hire Tess full-time. He knows she's good, and besides, that way he can make her life miserable."

"So you were engaged once before?" Jack asked, studying his half-eaten pie. He didn't want to admit that the thought bothered him.

"Nope, you're it for fiancés." She teasingly elbowed him in the ribs. "Craig and I were only eighteen at the time. It was never official."

Her smile faltered then. She glanced down at the ring nestled on the fourth finger of her left hand and Jack knew she was thinking that, for all the props and phony sentiments, this engagement wasn't official either.

"Yeah, but Craig is still mooning over her," Brian said. "And Mr. Applebee has never forgiven her for breaking his son's heart. The kid joined the Marines and hightailed it out of Pleasant River not long after he graduated from high school. Last I heard, he had re-upped for another six years."

Tess looked as if she could have cheerfully strangled her chatty brother-in-law.

"I didn't break his heart, Brian," she said through gritted teeth.

"Ah, Tess, darling, don't be so modest," Jack chided, enjoying the flush of irritation that stained her cheeks a lovely shade of pink. He draped a friendly arm over her shoulder and dropped a light kiss on the tip of her freckle-dusted nose. "Any man who lost you would be heartbroken."

As soon as the words left his mouth, he wanted to snatch them back. This time it was Jack who felt his face flush scarlet.

The Detroit Lions were losing fourteen to twenty-seven when Tess and Jack said their goodbyes and headed to the Fausts' home across town.

"Well, that went well," Tess said as the car pulled away from the curb. "I'm going shopping for a wedding dress tomorrow, and you'll be bonding with my brother-in-law at the local pub."

"There didn't seem to be any way to get out of it without raising a lot of eyebrows. I'm sorry," he said quietly.

"My God, Jack! My mother can't afford to buy a new dress for a wedding that won't take place."

"I know. I won't let it get that far," he promised. "Stall them tomorrow. Or, if you can't, only put down a deposit on the dress. I'll cover any non-refundable expenses after we tell everyone that we broke off our engagement."

She let out a weary breath and nodded. Then, "Speaking of our big breakup, when should it be?"

"I don't know."

"This afternoon served as a painful reminder that our lies can't go on indefinitely. The longer the charade continues, the more my family will suffer in the long run." Quietly, she added, "They like you, Jack."

He nodded. He was beginning to feel like the biggest heel. "I like them, too, Tess."

"So, when should we break up?" she persisted.

"I'm thinking we should at least wait until after Christmas. I don't want to appear to be some heartless cad."

A pair of finely arched brows inched up as she turned to look at him. "And who says you get to do the dumping?"

"I just figured it would be better if everyone blamed me."

"Blamed you for what? Breaking my heart. Oh, that would be just great," she sniffed. "Then I can walk around town with everyone I know giving me pitying stares and talking behind their hands about how that stud Jack Maris tossed me over because I wasn't good enough for him."

She had worked up a fine head of steam, and it gave him a glimpse of the temper that was rumored to go along with red hair. She sure was adorable when she was mad.

"Well, I guess you can be the dumper. I'll be the dumpee," he offered in sham seriousness.

"Oh, that's much better!" she hollered, and gestured with gloved hands. "I can see it now. Half the female population of Pleasant River will be rushing to your side to offer aid and comfort. And I'll be vilified as the conniving woman who encouraged you to relocate to the Midwest so we could be together only to give you the heave-ho once you got here."

She crossed her arms over her chest and glared at him.

"Stud, huh?" When her eyes narrowed into dangerous little gray slits, he returned his full attention to the road.

He let her seethe in silence for a couple of blocks, then he couldn't resist asking, "Tess, are we having our first fight?"

"No," she responded frostily, but a moment later he thought he saw her shoulders start to shake. Then an unladylike snort rent the air. "I guess we are," she admitted between giggles. "And over who will dump whom, no less."

"So, have you decided which you'd rather be? The jilted bride or the heartless fiancée? I'm flexible."

"Keep it up, Maris, and I'll become the grieving fiancée whose intended met with a grisly end."

The party was going full tilt when Tess and Jack stepped onto the porch of the Fausts' stately, columned home. They could hear music and laughter coming from inside, but Tess didn't feel particularly festive as she prepared to give yet another public performance as the happy fiancée.

She heard Jack take a couple of deep breaths. "Ready?"

She nodded and he rang the bell. Moments later they had been relieved of their coats, and the Fausts were greeting them warmly.

"It's so nice to see you both again," Cora said. "Everyone here is talking about your engagement. I'm afraid it didn't stay a secret very long." She batted her eyes innocently.

Tess managed a wan smile. "Oh, that's all right. We knew everyone would find out eventually." She allowed herself a moment to imagine how much less complicated her life would be if only Cora Faust knew how to keep a secret.

"Your mother is absolutely thrilled," Cora confided. She turned to Jack. "She thinks you're wonderful. Handsome, kind, very devoted to her daughter. She told me as much last week at the beauty shop. 'He's quite the catch,' she said."

"Really? And here I thought I was the lucky one," he replied, sending Tess a wink.

"Hey, Jack! About time you got here," a man called from across the room. He was sandy-haired and handsome in an all-American sort of way. And something about his ready smile and warm eyes made Tess relax as he made his way over, offering apologies to the people he jostled out of the way as he crossed the crowded room. When he reached them, he grabbed Jack's hand and pumped it enthusiastically. Gesturing to the petite blonde who had followed him through the throng of guests, he said, "We were wondering if you were going to show."

"Hey, beautiful," Jack said, kissing the woman on one smooth cheek. "You remember Tess." Because the Fausts still stood within earshot, he added, "The love of my life."

Jack drew Tess forward, resting a familiar hand on the small of her back. It seemed to sear her skin through the clingy fabric of her dress.

"We'll have to invite Davis and Marianne to the house for dinner after the wedding," he said, surreptitiously supplying the names of his friends for Tess. She caught Davis's wink and realized they were in on the ruse.

When the Fausts moved out of earshot, Tess glanced around. She knew many of the guests. In a town the size of Pleasant River, people got to know one another, if not well, then at least by sight. That was something Jack's big-city background hadn't prepared him for when he'd asked her to pose as his fiancée. Many of the guests were openly curious about seeing Tess and the new vice president of Faust Enterprises out together at a social function for the first time.

"People are staring," she whispered.

"Yes, it would seem you and Jack are the star attractions," Marianne agreed dryly.

"The last time I felt this conspicuous, I was ten and Sister Agatha made me sit in the corner for chewing gum in class."

Marianne snickered. "Well, you can thank my husband for your discomfort. He's the one who put this harebrained idea in Jack's head in the first place."

"Oh, really?"

Davis smiled innocently and apparently decided it best to beat a hasty retreat. "Jack, why don't we go get Marianne and the future Mrs. Maris a drink?"

* * *

"Well, I have to hand it to you," Davis told Jack as they poured their drinks. "Despite the short notice you sure managed to snag yourself one fine-looking woman." He whistled low and shook his head. "Waking up next to her every morning wouldn't be any trouble." He slanted Jack a look brimming with speculation. "Of course, maybe you already know that."

Jack felt his temper rise. He couldn't say why his friend's crude comment made him so angry, any more than he could keep from growling, "It's not like that, Davis. *She's* not like that."

Irritation warred with irony. Funny, he thought, but just the other night, he had wanted Tess to be like that, willing to sleep with him, eager to tear up the sheets until they were both too sweaty and exhausted to do anything more laborious than smile and breathe. He still wanted that. Still woke up aroused in the morning from dreaming about it. But Davis made it sound cheap and tawdry. He made Tess sound cheap and tawdry. Jack knew better than most people did that neither description applied.

His irritation must have shown on his face, because Davis took a step back and raised his hands in apology.

"Sorry," he said, sounding appropriately contrite. Then he spoiled the effect by laughing. "Pardon me for asking, Jack, but if you're not interested, what's wrong with you? The woman is built like a goddess, and she isn't bad from the neck up, either. If I were single…" He cast out the thought and even though Jack knew he was being baited, he bit anyway. The anger and jealousy he felt were nearly instantaneous.

"Don't even think about it, pal." Violence simmered in his blood, potent and primal. When he noticed the gleam in Davis's eyes, he tried to recover quickly. "I mean, Marianne would have your hide if you so much as looked at another woman."

Davis nodded, seeming unconvinced and thoroughly enjoying his best friend's discomfort. "No doubt she wouldn't be the only one seeking a pound of my flesh. But my wife does let me look, and what I see is one beautiful woman."

Jack gazed across the room to where Tess stood chatting companionably with Marianne. She had worn her hair up tonight, pulled into an intricate French braid with just a few wisps of fire curling about her face. The emerald dress that followed her sleek curves was simple but elegant, and it made his mouth water just to look at her.

"She is beautiful," he agreed. But how could he explain to Davis that Tess was also smart and funny, ambitious and loyal, kind and warm-hearted. She was willing to stick to a promise she'd made to a stranger, even when doing so pitched her neatly ordered life into absolute chaos. Beautiful, Jack knew, didn't begin to sum up Tess Donovan. The reasons he thought about her day and night went much deeper than that. And they scared him, because he knew he wasn't the kind of man capable of giving someone like her what she needed to be truly happy.

"I had a nice time today, Tess. Especially with your family. Thanks," Jack said as he drove her home just after midnight. Tess sat beside him, sleepy in the warm confines of his sports coupe. The leather bucket seat hugged her like a lover, making her feel relaxed and safe.

"You're welcome. I liked having you there. Did you miss your family today?"

He laughed a little harshly, and at first she didn't think he would answer. Then he said, "My family's Thanksgivings were never that—let's just say, they were never that peaceful."

"You've never told me much about your folks, although I gather they're divorced." She stifled a yawn with the palm of her hand, before continuing. "What are they like?"

"What are they like?" he repeated. "Well, my father lives in Oak Park, Illinois, with his fifth wife, Amanda. Mandy for short," he said with a derisive snort. "She's only a couple of years older than me."

"Ah, the trophy wife," Tess said.

"Trophy wife number four, actually," he corrected. "And the older he gets, the younger they get." He turned to Tess and, with an eyebrow arched, said sardonically, "He and Mandy had a baby a while back. I have a half-brother who is four."

"Oh, my." Tess blinked.

"Yeah, that's the PG version of my reaction when Dad told me she was pregnant." He chuckled a little, but the sound held only bitterness. She wondered if he realized how wounded he was, as she listened to the rest of his grim recitation.

"Anyway, Janice is on husband number four."

"Janice?"

"My mother. Her latest husband manages a ski resort in Aspen. Doug's about ten years her junior. They met a few years ago while she was still married to Doug's brother. I don't see her much. I haven't seen her much, in fact, for the past twenty years. Dad got custody of my older sister and me. My mother didn't

want to be bothered with us after the divorce. I think
I've spent exactly eight Thanksgivings with Janice in
all those years. The rest of the time I was with Dad,
who played musical girlfriends when he wasn't playing musical wives.''

"That must have been hard on you."

He made a little noise in the back of his throat,
neither accepting nor denying her words.

"No harder, I'd imagine, than losing your dad. Not
as hard, in fact, since I still got to see my mother
from time to time. I just don't have much in common
with her."

Tess tried to imagine not seeing her mother for
months at a stretch. The two women didn't always
see eye to eye, but she knew she would be lost without Rita. How sad, she thought, that Jack didn't enjoy
a close relationship with either parent.

"What about your sister?" she asked softly. Surely
he had to be close to someone.

"Kirsten?" He rolled his shoulders in dismissal.
"She lives near L.A. She's an assistant prosecutor,
very bright, very driven. We talk on the phone now
and then, but I don't get out to the West Coast much,
and she's never been to Boston."

"Does she have any children?"

"No. I don't think she wants any. She's got a high-
powered, high-pressure career. There wasn't even
time for her husband, let alone kids. She's divorced
now, anyway." He glanced over at Tess. "In case
you're keeping score, that's three for three in my family. You may have noticed that the Marises aren't
particularly good at keeping their commitments."

Jack maneuvered the car to a stop in front of Tess's

home. As he shifted into Park, she asked softly, "What about your grandmother?"

The question seemed to catch him off guard. "My grandmother?"

Tess tugged off her glove and held out her left hand. Even in the automobile's dim interior, the ring's marquis-cut diamond twinkled like something celestial.

"Ah, Grandmother Maris." For the first time while discussing his family, a truly affectionate smile made his lips curve. "The old gal died a year ago at eighty-five. She outlived her husband of fifty-seven years by a mere six months." Sounding perplexed, he added, "I think she died of a broken heart."

"She must have loved your grandfather very much."

"Adored him. Even his faults." His genuine bafflement at something so basic saddened Tess. How could anyone not know that true love was unconditional?

"That's the way it's supposed to be when you're in love. Maybe when you finally get married, you'll take after her."

"Maybe," he agreed as he yanked open the car door. Before slamming it shut, he added matter-of-factly, "But I don't intend ever to find out."

Chapter Six

Tess hadn't realized a day of dress shopping could be so emotionally taxing. She, of course, was the only Donovan woman who felt that way. Her mother and sister were enjoying themselves immensely. Rita went with the apricot dress she'd mentioned at dinner the day before. Betsy chose a full-length satin sheath in pale yellow. The saleswoman measured them, ordered their dresses in the appropriate sizes, and then the trio turned to Tess, looking expectant and hopeful. But she purposely avoided the racks of bridal gowns. She felt like too much of a fraud to look at them, even as her fingers itched to touch the delicate lace sewn onto silk and satin.

"I've got my heart set on one I saw in a bridal magazine," she fibbed. The saleswoman, being ever so helpful, brought over a stack of the latest volumes.

"If it's in one of these we either have it in stock or we can order it," she announced cheerfully. The woman was fortyish, blond, and had *perky* all but stamped on her forehead. But she was only being helpful, Tess knew. And since she reminded Tess of June Cleaver on "Leave it to Beaver" she found it hard to dislike the woman. Who, after all, could hate the Beav's mom?

Tess was flipping half-heartedly through the pages of the sixth magazine when she spotted it. Her busy fingers stilled, and she forgot her clever plan to pretend not to find the dress of her dreams within the magazine's pages.

"Oh, Tess, is that it?" Betsy chirped, peering over Tess's shoulder to get a better look. Rita stopped hunting through a selection of dyeable satin pumps and hurried over to do the same.

Tess didn't know what possessed her, but she said, "This is the dress I've always pictured myself getting married in."

And it was true. As a girl she might not have been able to imagine the face of her prospective groom, but the dress she had known in detail. And there it was on the page before her.

"Well, you're in luck," the saleswoman beamed. "We have that one." She looked Tess over with a practiced eye. "The one we have in stock is in a size ten, but I can pin you into it, and if you like it, we'll order it in the appropriate size."

Five minutes later Tess found herself in a fitting room, wearing a crinoline. As she pulled yards of lace-trimmed ivory satin over her head, she became as caught up in the excitement of planning her make-believe wedding as her mother and sister were.

"Do you have it on yet?" Betsy called from outside the fitting room. Tess had insisted on going inside with only the saleswoman to help her. The woman was busily tucking in the extra folds of fabric with straight pins she pulled from between her compressed lips.

"I'll be out in a minute, Bets."

Tess couldn't take her eyes off her reflection. The dress shimmered in the room's bright lighting. It had small beaded cap sleeves that barely extended past her shoulders and a lacy bodice that hugged her slender torso now that the saleswoman had secured it into place. Tess turned to one side and then the other in front of the full-length mirror, admiring the billowing ivory skirt and chapel-length train the saleswoman stretched out behind her. She looked like a princess, she thought, feeling a little giddy. And she felt like Cinderella as she slipped her feet inside the delicate ivory satin shoes the saleswoman had brought into the fitting room for her.

"Let me help you with the veil," the woman offered. "Will you be wearing your hair up?"

"Y-yes, I think so," Tess stammered. In all her girlhood dreams about her wedding day, she had worn her hair up. Tess reached into her purse and pulled out a large clip. Gathering up the thick mass of curls, she secured it at her nape, and then stood speechless as the saleswoman placed the simple veil atop her head as if performing a coronation.

"You'll make a beautiful bride," the saleswoman said, admiring Tess in the full-length mirror.

Tess nodded stiffly as every girlhood fantasy paraded through her mind. She could almost hear the wedding march and smell the orange blossoms. Then her eyes filled with tears that spilled down her cheeks. She batted them away with the backs of her hands, but they just kept coming, coursing downward in a silent, salty waterfall of misery that the saleswoman mistook for feminine sentimentality. The Beav's mother fished a neatly folded tissue out of her sweater pocket and handed it to Tess.

"I'm s-sorry," Tess hiccuped, more than a little embarrassed. She wasn't sure what she was apologizing for exactly, or why she was apologizing to the saleswoman. She figured she owed a lot of people an apology, and the two most obvious candidates were waiting just outside the door, eager to see Tess in her June finery. The thought made her cry even harder.

"It's okay, hon," the woman assured Tess, giving her arm a little pat of understanding. "A lot of young women cry the first time they try on their wedding dress."

"Tess! Come on," Betsy pleaded impatiently from the other side of the door. "Mom and I are dying to see you in that dress. Open up, already."

Tess swiped at the tears with the tissue, offered the saleswoman a watery smile, and braced herself for her family's reaction. When the door swung open, she heard Rita and Betsy gasp simultaneously.

"It's perfect, Tess. Just perfect," Betsy sighed.

"Oh, honey, you're just a picture," Rita sniffed, as she wrapped her arms around her younger daughter and squeezed gently. Into Tess's ear she whispered, "I wish your daddy were here to see you. I know he'd be so proud to walk you down the aisle."

"Oh, Mom," Tess wailed, eyes welling up again. Rita and Betsy began crying in earnest as well.

Rita reached up to brush away Tess's tears. "But I know your father would be pleased with your choice of husband. He'd like Jack, I know he would. He wanted you to marry a man you love. I look at you when Jack's in the room, the way your eyes light up and you get all flustered, and I know my baby girl is head over heels. That's how I was with your daddy,'' Rita confided, nostalgia making her voice thick. ''It's truly all a parent can want for their child. Love might not take care of everything in a marriage, but it sure makes solving problems that much easier.''

To which Tess blubbered, ''I really do love Jack Maris, Mom. I really do.''

Skip's Pub catered to an eclectic crowd. Near the front of the bar, those who thought they could carry a tune, or who were too drunk to care that they couldn't, were crooning to the beat of the karaoke machine. A busty middle-aged woman, poured into a pair of jeans about two sizes too small, was singing an ear-splitting rendition of Madonna's ''Like a Virgin.'' As she swiveled her fleshy hips, several rowdy and randy mechanics wearing grease-stained work shirts shouted their appreciation.

In the back, a trio of flannel-clad old men was lined up on bar stools swapping stories about farm implements and commiserating about corn prices as they sipped their beers.

Jack found himself wedged between those two alien worlds, at first feeling sort of homesick for the posh, upscale drinking establishments he had frequented in Boston. But the longer he and Brian sat at a small wooden table that had an obscene word etched into its sticky top, the more he liked the place. It had a kind of homespun charm that grew on him. Their table was located in the midst of a handful of other tables that were occupied by diehard Detroit Red

Wings fans, who had all come to watch the game on Skip's 52-inch television.

"I want one of these monsters for the house," Brian admitted around a mouthful of salty popcorn. His gaze regarding the large-screen TV was similar to the gazes of the mechanics as they regarded the Madonna wannabe.

"I bought one a couple of years ago." Jack flashed him a smug grin. "Nancy nearly hyperventilated when I brought the thing home." He chuckled at the memory, before catching the look of brotherly concern that had Brian's eyebrows tugging together.

"Nancy?"

Jack ran his tongue over his teeth and grimaced. No graceful way out of this one, he thought. He faced the man who clearly thought of himself as Tess's protector since she didn't have a father or older brother. Jack admired him for that. And, in truth, he liked Brian. The guy was honest, sincere. Jack felt a twinge of regret that the two probably wouldn't be on speaking terms once the "engagement" ended.

"Um, she's an ex-girlfriend. We lived together in Boston." When Brian continued to stare at him, as if trying to puzzle things out, Jack added. "Before I met Tess."

Brian nodded slowly, appearing somewhat satisfied with the explanation. "Well, I guess we all have a past, huh? Tess knows about her, though, right?"

Jack had already consumed two beers and a celebratory shot of whiskey that the man at the next table had insisted on buying for all the hockey fans when the Wings scored their first goal. He wasn't drunk precisely; he was just pleasantly fuzzy. Too fuzzy to keep track of more lies. So, with a sigh he admitted, "No, I've never told Tess about Nancy."

Disapproval edged Brian's expression. "That's no way to start a marriage, trust me. You should tell Tess about this as soon as possible. A woman likes to know when the man she's about to marry once shared living quarters with another female."

"I haven't been intentionally deceitful. It's just never come up," Jack said defensively. Then he blurted, "I didn't know till last night that Tess had once been all but engaged to that Craig Applebee character."

A slow grin spread across Brian's face. "You're not jealous?"

Jack started to shake his head. He wasn't jealous. That would mean he had to truly care about Tess as more than just a friend, and he didn't. He couldn't. Marises just weren't cut out for handling the baggage that came along with those kinds of emotions. And Tess wasn't like Nancy—or like he'd thought Nancy was: content with the status quo, understanding his limitations in the commitment department.

But the denial never made it past his lips. Instead, alcohol, and what he refused to recognize as sexual frustration, had him growling, "Yes, I'm jealous! I don't like to think of Tess with anyone but me."

He slumped back in his chair after he said it, amazed that he had done so. Still, it felt good to admit it, he thought, and took a swig of beer. Then he felt honor-bound to report to Brian, "Not that I've been *with* Tess."

Of all the reactions he might have expected that announcement to elicit from the self-appointed protector of Tess's virtue, the wide grin and unrestrained shout of laughter were not it.

"I owe Betsy five bucks," Brian announced, struggling to rein in his hilarity.

"Excuse me?"

"Oh, don't get all offended. It's nothing to be ashamed of. In fact, I respect the fact that you two decided to wait," he said sincerely, then laughed even louder.

Jack hunched forward, and in a small voice asked, "What does this have to do with Betsy and five bucks?" He had a queasy feeling he didn't really want to know.

"Well, uh, my wife mentioned that Tess had been awfully moody lately, and she noticed the way you two were eyeing one another at dinner yesterday. You both had a feast in mind, but it wasn't the one on the table." He wiggled his eyebrows meaningfully and Jack squirmed in his chair.

"Anyway, Betsy said the problem was sex, or the lack of it. I thought it might be more basic, like money or wedding plan conflicts with your family being from out of town and all."

"And you and your wife wagered on it," Jack surmised.

"It's all in good fun," Brian assured him, and smacked him solidly on the back. "I give you credit, Jack. Bets and I didn't wait. She was living with her folks back then, too, which made for some interesting—" he cut off the sentence with an embarrassed chuckle. "Anyway, if Betsy had lived in her own apartment like Tess, or if I'd had my own place, gosh, I don't think we would have gotten a lick of sleep during the months before our wedding. You two must have wills of steel," he marveled.

"Yeah, well," Jack ran a hand around the back of his neck and grumbled, "I'm not getting a whole lot of sleep as it is."

"Less than seven months to go," Brian reminded him. He hoisted his bottle of beer and tapped it against the one in Jack's hand. "Here's to chastity," he toasted solemnly, then he started laughing all over again.

Two hours later, Brian helped Jack stagger into the parking lot. After their chat on premarital sex, it had become clear that Jack was intent on overindulging. Brian had switched to cola and managed to discreetly divest Jack of his keys.

"I think you'd better leave your car here. I'll drive you home," Brian said, motioning toward an older-model Ford truck with Hopper Construction painted on the side.

Jack didn't seem inclined to argue. He changed course with an abrupt turn, lurching unsteadily toward the pickup. Brian scurried after him, grabbing his arm just in time to save him from falling flat on his face in the gravel parking lot.

"You're going to have one heck of a headache in the morning," Brian said under his breath as he helped Jack into the truck. He chuckled unsympathetically as he jogged around to the driver's side. "But from my point of view it was worth it."

After several drinks, the conversation had turned decidedly entertaining. Clearly, Jack was besotted with Tess, and sexually frustrated beyond the point of all sanity. After going over all of the reasons Tess would make a perfect wife, he kept mumbling about tangled webs and defective genes and how he wished he could be more like his Grandmother Maris. Not much of it made sense to Brian, but the main message came through loud and clear: the man was stupid in love. And that made Brian like him all the more.

"Hey, let's drive past Tess's house," Jack said as Brian reached over to buckle his inebriated passenger's seat belt. Jack's slurred speech made the sentence come out as one word.

Brian doubted Jack would still be conscious by the time he dropped him off at the Saint Sebastian, let alone able to first visit with Tess at her home. "I don't think so. It's after midnight, and she's probably in bed."

That announcement earned him a throaty groan. Jack's head slumped sideways on the headrest and, with glassy eyes, he gazed pathetically at Brian. "Do you really think so?"

When Brian nodded, Jack added in a wistful garble, "I wonder what she wears to bed. I'm figuring her for a prim little nightie with rosebuds all over it." He smiled a dopey grin and admitted with all the unabashed earnestness of a drunk, "But I'm fantasizing about a black teddy."

Brian grinned and shook his head. As he started the engine he said, half to himself, "I'll just bet you are."

When Brian put on his left blinker at the first light, Jack sputtered, "Hey, that's not the way to Tess's house. Come on, be a pal, drive me over there. If you don't I'll just have to get someone at the hotel to do it."

Brian had the uncomfortable feeling that if Jack were conscious when he arrived back at the hotel he would do just that. After a moment's indecision, he decided he would save Tess the gossip by heeding Jack's wishes. After all, he doubted that Jack would be up to seduction in his present state.

"Whatever you say, Jack," he replied, turning the truck in the opposite direction.

The windows in Tess's upstairs apartment were dark when Brian pulled up in front of the old brick house. He managed to half drag, half carry Jack onto the porch, then he rang the bell and waited. The porch light flickered on as the neighbor's dog began yapping, and then Tess appeared, wearing a hastily belted robe, her hair rumpled from sleep. She opened the door and urged them both inside with a frantic wave of her hand.

"What on earth happened to him?" she hissed, when Jack, propped up by Brian, managed only a lopsided grin and shaky wave hello.

"I'm afraid he's had a few too many," Brian said, trying to look contrite and failing miserably.

"And why, pray tell, have you brought him here?"

"Aw, Tess, aren't you glad to see me?" Jack wailed. His bellow had the dog barking again.

"Shhhh!" Tess admonished. "You'll wake up the neighbors." With a sigh of defeat, she turned and plodded up the stairs, motioning for Brian to follow behind her with Jack.

Inside the apartment, Brian deposited Jack onto her couch and turned to go.

"You're not leaving him here, are you?" Tess asked, looking both incredulous and unnerved. "I mean, he can't possibly stay here all night." Her voice cracked as she added in what sounded like a hopeful whisper, "Brian, we're not married yet."

"That's half the poor slob's problem," he muttered, sparing a glance at the snoring man sprawled on Tess's couch. "I don't think you need to worry about him making any advances tonight. About the only thing likely to rise on Jack is the contents of his stomach."

After imparting that cheery thought, Brian opened the door and left. He was halfway down the steps when he turned around and winked at Tess, who stood in the open doorway staring after him with a stricken look on her face. "Be gentle with him, eh? June's a lifetime away for a man in his condition."

Tess didn't have long to ponder her brother-in-law's puzzling words. From behind her, she heard a heavy thud followed by a creative curse. She turned around to find more than six feet and one hundred and eighty pounds of drunken man face down on her flowered rug. Jack had apparently rolled off her couch, taking half of her decorative throw pillows with him. They were scattered around him on the floor like large, colorful pieces of confetti.

"Jack!" She knelt beside him and gave his arm a vigorous shake. "Are you all right?"

He made a muffled sound that she couldn't quite decipher. After several labored attempts, she managed to roll him onto his back, where he lay very still with his eyes shut. She had to admit he looked terribly vulnerable lying on her floor, his face pale and pinched. Vulnerable, but very male, she amended, taking note of the day's growth of whiskers that shadowed his jaw. She ran her fingers through his tawny hair, indulging in a little fantasy of her own. It was softer than she had expected.

"Mmm, that feels good," he mumbled. He opened glassy eyes and squinted up at her.

"You have the face of an angel." His gaze didn't stay on her face, though. It traveled down the exposed length of her throat to the triangle of pink cotton that was visible where her robe parted. "No rosebuds, no black teddy," he murmured.

"I think we need to get you to bed," she said, trying to be all efficient while her heart hammered and her body heated under his hungry gaze. She might not understand the meaning behind his words, but the direction his thoughts had taken became very obvious.

"That's where I want to be, in your bed." He reached up with an unsteady hand to cup her cheek, stroking the pad of his thumb over her parted lips. "With you, Tess," he whispered thickly, his words slurred, but his meaning clear.

"Jack, we've been over this before, I—"

He cut off her words by rolling his head furiously side to side on the carpet. "I can't marry you, Tess." He sounded so sad when he said it that her heart tripped a little.

"I know."

"No, you don't understand. I won't marry anyone. It just wouldn't work. I can't promise you more than an exclusive dating relationship for as long as it lasts. But I want to be with you. I *really* want to be with you. Only you, Tess."

His hand snaked around to the back of her neck, tugging her head down to his. Yes, Tess thought, her answer would be yes this time. Even if she could have him for just a little while. Even if it all meant so much more to her than to him, it would be worth it. Forget her pride, she wanted to be with him. To feel him stretched out over her, hard muscle melting into soft curves, loving her even if only in the physical sense of the word.

She intended to seal her unspoken decision with a kiss, but a second after it began she felt Jack's lips go slack and heard his breathing grow deep and even.

Tess sat back on her haunches and gazed down at his peacefully slumbering face. *Should I be insulted or amused,* she wondered, *that my seducer has fallen asleep in mid-seduction?* She leaned down and kissed him lightly on the mouth.

"What am I going to do about you, Jack Maris?" she murmured.

Chapter Seven

Jack awoke with a start, the first shrill ring of the telephone cleaving his head nearly in two. The second had his bloodshot eyes rolling back in their sandpaper sockets. With a groan he fought to free his hands from the mound of tangled blankets that wrapped him more securely than a mummy's rags. The phone pealed one more time before he could snatch the receiver from its cradle on the end table, making him even more irritable.

"Yeah!" he barked, using the same tone that caused telemarketers to hang up without ever offering a sales pitch.

Silence hummed on the line for a moment, then, to his profound chagrin, Tess's mother's voice came across as clear as the day outside and her tone twice as chilly.

"Jack, I'd like to speak to Tess, please."

His brain fog cleared immediately, and he realized that he was in Tess's apartment, sprawled on her couch, and, based on the jeans and other articles of his clothing strewn about the room, wearing very little. But while he didn't remember exactly what had transpired between Tess and him, he did remember undressing at some point and climbing under the blankets she'd left on the couch. And, he knew he hadn't made love to her. Hungover or not, he would feel a lot better if he had.

"Um, good morning, Mrs. Donovan. Sorry to have been so rude, it's just that the phone woke…uh, Tess is…I think I hear the shower running…." Every word he uttered seemed more damning than the last. Finally he said, "Can I take a message for her?"

"I just wanted to invite her, well both of you actually, to Sunday brunch tomorrow after mass."

"I'll give her the message, ma'am," he replied politely before hanging up.

Next to the phone he spied a crystal bowl full of peppermints. His mouth was dry as dust so he unwrapped one red-and-white-striped candy and popped it into his mouth, savoring it for a minute. *What I'd give for a toothbrush and a little mouthwash,* he thought, but he settled for a couple more mints. After winning another wrestling match with the covers, he finally managed to stumble to his feet.

A squeaking of floorboards caught his attention. There stood Tess, wrapped in a thick terrycloth robe, a towel turban on her head. She looked away with a guilty start, but it took only a glimpse of her reddened face to remind Jack that he was wearing only his jockey shorts and, for some reason, one blue sock.

"How are you feeling this morning?" she asked, her gaze fixed on some point just beyond his left shoulder.

He retrieved his jeans from the floor and had them pulled halfway up one leg before he answered in a raspy voice, "I've been better."

While Jack tugged denim over his lean hips and worked up the zipper, Tess dared to boldly study him. He sure was gorgeous. Dark hair sprinkled his muscular chest and trailed down his flat abdomen, disappearing inside the waistband of his jeans. As she stared, fascinated, the wall clock began to chime.

Jack gave up trying to dress, clamping his hands over his ears instead. "What in God's name is that racket?" he cried.

"Racket?" Tess repeated, then it dawned on her. "Ah, the clock. It's nine a.m."

"Why would anyone own something that noisy?" he asked in a hushed tone, as if not wanting to risk an aneurysm.

She raised an eyebrow and said dryly, "Oh, on most mornings I doubt this would bother you."

"Yeah, well, between that and the phone, I'm lucky my skull hasn't shattered yet."

"Phone?"

He found his shirt under a pile of throw pillows and shrugged into it. "Your, uh, mom called."

Tess sputtered incoherently before squeaking, "My mother? Please tell me you let the machine pick it up?"

Jack ducked his chin and became absorbed in buttoning his shirt. Tess noticed he had missed the first one so the entire thing was off by one button from collar to wrinkled hem. She stared at the crooked job while she waited for him to respond.

Finally, he said defensively, "I didn't mean to answer it, but it was ringing and I just didn't think about where I was or who it might be.''

When she only made a strangled little noise in response, he added, ''She invited us to brunch tomorrow after church.''

''Did you tell her you'd just stopped by?'' Tess's mood brightened and she nodded excitedly. ''That's it! Tomorrow we'll casually mention that you were out for a run and came up for coffee.''

''Yeah, that would work, except...''

''Except what?''

''Well, I mentioned that she woke me up,'' he admitted sheepishly.

She couldn't believe this. It had been bad enough when Jack implied to Cora Faust that he and Tess were intimate. She didn't want to think about the impression Jack had left with her mother. Thank God she had just called and not come over.

''What else did you mention?'' Tess asked, hands on hips.

''Just that you were in the shower, and I'd give you the message.''

''Great,'' she gritted out between clenched teeth. ''Why didn't you just tell her she was interrupting something hot and sweaty, and that I'd call her back when we were through?''

He looked up, a smile already forming on his lips. She flattened her eyes into little slits of warning and he swallowed any suggestive remark he may have been considering.

Tess watched as Jack began to work the tails of his misbuttoned and iron-challenged shirt into his jeans. No doubt he intended to leave now that he had made such an incalculable mess of her life. She stalked forward, determined to at least see that he left her apartment looking presentable.

"Oh, please," she said, batting his hands away. "Let me. I don't want you walking out of here looking as if you were in such a rush to leave after spending the night that you couldn't even get your clothes back on right."

She began to undo his shirt, nimble fingers making fast work of the first three buttons, and then they slowed as she realized how intimate the task appeared.

"You do the rest," she said curtly, even though her fingers itched to finish the job. There was something decidedly sexy about unbuttoning a man's shirt, leaning the heels of her hands against the firm expanse of his chest. The shirt still smelled of his cologne and a little bit of cigarette smoke from the bar. And his breath smelled suspiciously like peppermints.

"Tess." The word came out half prayer, half question. His hands moved to her hips, pulling them into close proximity with his own. The evidence of his arousal was unmistakable, but as if he thought she might doubt it, he trailed a few light kisses over her cheek to her ear, where he whispered, "I seem to be like this a lot lately."

She closed her eyes, acutely aware that she wore nothing under her bathrobe. He seemed to have figured that out, too. His hands loosened the knotted belt, then slipped inside, roaming over her flesh in a tender caress.

He pushed the robe onto her shoulders and stared, then said thickly, "You are too beautiful for words, Tess." He nuzzled her neck and then bent to trail reverent kisses over her collarbone and down her shoulder.

"Jack," she moaned when he flicked a thumb over her hardened nipple. "Jack, I don't think…"

"That's right, sweetheart, don't think," he said between kisses. "That's half our problem. We both think too much."

He had a point, she decided, her body so inflamed by desire she didn't bother to question whether it was hormones or her head that had reached that conclusion. She tugged his shirt open and ran her hands over his tautly muscled chest, experiencing a thrilling sense of power when he sucked in a ragged breath. She'd never touched a man so intimately before, or been touched so intimately herself.

His shirt and her robe hit the floor at the same time, as she and Jack came together in a maddeningly frantic kiss. All maidenly tentativeness left Tess as her blood heated past the boiling point. Their hands seemed to be everywhere, streaking across each other's skin—touching, stroking and caressing. Their mouths followed—tasting, nibbling and feasting greedily on bared flesh. Tess couldn't seem to get close enough, especially not with him wearing those jeans. Jack apparently read her mind.

Their fingers were tangled together, tugging feverishly at his jammed zipper when the doorbell pealed. Like boxers in a ring, they immediately stepped away from each other, retreating to their respective corners as they waited for sanity to return.

"Please, tell me someone's not standing on your doorstep at nine on a Saturday morning," he said, his breathing labored.

Tess retrieved her discarded robe from the floor and

struggled into it before flying to the window to sneak a peek through the blinds. Across the street, she recognized Brian's truck parked at the curb.

"It seems your ride has arrived," she said, equally breathless. She turned and looked at him, noting the heavy-lidded gaze, bare torso, half-undone jeans, and the telltale bulge of his arousal straining against denim. Clearing her throat, she advised diplomatically, "I think you'd, um, better make yourself presentable while I go answer the door."

Jack listened to her footsteps on the stairs and smiled. He could have told Tess that her robe was on inside out, the towel on her head was askew, and that she looked like she had just been kissed to within an inch of an orgasm, but he decided not to make her more self-conscious than she probably already was.

A minute later, Brian and Betsy followed Tess up the stairs. Betsy greeted Jack with a cheerful smile and pretended nothing was amiss. Her husband, however, sent Jack a smug look that told him he knew exactly what he and Betsy had interrupted with their ill-timed visit. He smiled most annoyingly and said a little louder than was necessary, "Great morning, eh, Jack?"

Jack cringed, his eyes watering as his headache throbbed back to life. He had donned his shirt, but thought it best to leave it untucked for the moment, his jeans just a little too revealing given his condition. "Yeah, terrific."

"I thought I'd come take you home, save Tess the trip," Brian explained, again a few decibels louder than was called for. "Bets came along for the ride."

"Good grief, Bri, could you keep it down," Tess admonished. "We're not hard-of-hearing."

"Sorry." He ducked his head, but not quite in time to hide his grin. "I didn't realize."

"Have any coffee?" Betsy asked, smiling sweetly.

"I haven't made any yet," Tess replied, looking flustered and, Jack thought, quite adorable in her inside-out bathrobe. Still, he felt a little guilty about his part in her discomfort. Since she'd met him, it seemed Tess found herself in awkward situations with surprising frequency. Yet, she was trying to make the most of this one.

Acting the gracious hostess, she said, "Please, make yourselves at home while I make a pot."

Then she turned and caught sight of the room. Jack watched her suck her lower lip between her teeth. The couch was covered with blankets, the floor littered with throw pillows, and one blue sock hung from the lampshade. Tess looked as if she wanted to scream or cry, but only a hysterical little giggle escaped, which she smothered with a cough.

Betsy at last took pity on her.

"I'll brew the coffee. Why don't you go get dressed."

Alone in her room, Tess took one look at herself in the full-length mirror on the back of the closet door and slapped a hand over her mouth to keep an anguished wail from escaping. A person would have to be blind not to figure out that she and Jack had been going at each other like a couple of oversexed teenagers. Her cheeks were flushed, the skin around her lips chapped from his beard stubble. She opened her robe, which to her mortification was inside out, and gasped. As she pulled on a pair of panties and a bra, she thanked her lucky stars that no one could see the whisker burns on her breasts.

The towel on her head was leaning like the famous Tower of Pisa. She took it off and began untangling her hair. She was bent over, working her fingers through the damp mass, when someone knocked on her door. She didn't have time to call "come in" before Jack entered.

Jack needed to talk to Tess, but he very nearly forgot his own name when he walked in and saw her. She straightened, giving him a good view of long slender legs, gently rounded hips and a small, nipped-in waist. One look was all it took to convince him that black teddies were overrated. Tess looked sexy as all get out in serviceable white cotton, her wet hair falling around her shoulders like festive streamers. The sight of her made him wish they could simply close the bedroom door, lock out the pesky interruptions and pick up where they had left off.

"Jack! What are you doing in here?" she snatched up the robe from her bed and held it in front of her, looking shy despite the fact that he had seen her wearing nothing at all not more than fifteen minutes ago.

"Torturing myself," he muttered thickly. Then, "Tess, I need to speak to you alone for a minute before Brian drags me out of here. What went on before your family showed up at your door, does that mean you've changed your mind about...about... us?"

She gave him an odd look, poignant somehow, as if there were something she was waiting for him to say. Finally, she replied, "Maybe...I don't know. I've never felt like this before, and when I'm with you, I can't seem to think straight."

"I'll take that as a compliment," he said, his gaze straying to the swell of creamy flesh visible above the robe she clutched to her bosom.

Her eyes narrowed. Apparently she knew him well enough to know what he was thinking. She backed up a step, putting more distance between them, and hastily shrugged into her robe.

"Jack." Her tone was a warning. "There are people in the next room. People who would have to be stupid not to know what we were doing before they arrived."

He swallowed hard and nodded, then turned to go. Before pulling the door shut behind him, he whispered, "Next time, I vote we don't answer when someone rings the bell."

Tess returned to the living room a few minutes later wearing faded jeans and a black turtleneck sweater, her still-damp hair caught back in a simple clip. She had applied some foundation to conceal the whisker burns, but the sly looks her brother-in-law and sister gave her told Tess she was fooling no one. Brian sat in the easy chair. Betsy and Jack shared the couch. Tess poured herself a mug of coffee and perched on the ottoman.

"So, did Mom call you about brunch tomorrow?" Betsy asked as they all sipped coffee and tried to ignore the tension fizzing around them.

"Yes, this morning. Will you and Brian be there?"

"Wouldn't miss it," Betsy replied around a smile that made Tess uneasy. "You guys going to nine o'clock mass with us before brunch or are you planning to go tonight?"

Tess gave Jack a helpless little look. It dawned on

her that she didn't even know if he was Catholic. "Uh, we'll be at the nine o'clock service," she said, hoping that was okay with him.

"So, did you tell Jack that you ordered your dress?" Betsy asked excitedly. She turned to Jack. "Mom and I ordered our dresses as well. But wait until you see Tess in hers. She is going to make the most beautiful bride."

Tess knew Jack was looking at her, but she couldn't meet his gaze. She stared instead at the inky liquid in her coffee mug.

"So, you ordered a dress?" he asked softly.

She cleared her throat, but her voice still came out in a pathetic little squeak. "Yes."

"It's really getting down to the wire, you know," Betsy piped in. "June's a busy month for weddings and there will be alterations to do. Tess has such a tiny waist, even ordered in her size, the gown will have to be taken in some and possibly hemmed." She took a sip of coffee and asked, "So, whom am I standing up with? Who's your best man, Jack?"

Jack stared at Tess's sister. The question surprised him, but no more than the response that slipped so effortlessly past his lips. "Davis Marx."

"I hope he's tall," Betsy said. "I want to wear heels with my dress."

"He's tall," Jack assured her.

"More coffee anyone?" Tess asked, hopping up as if eager to flee the room.

"Nah, we really should be going," Betsy said.

She and Brian were shrugging into their coats when Jack caught Tess by the arm and pulled her aside. After a quick, hard kiss, he whispered, "I'll call you later. I think we have a lot to talk about, and I'm not talking about the dress.''

"Hey, you ready, Jack?" Brian called.

Jack nodded, but he was looking at Tess when he replied, "I'm ready when you are."

The sun was setting outside, dropping the temperature well below freezing. Tess sat curled up in an afghan on the couch, surrounded by notes and textbooks, trying to do some early studying for final exams, but all she had managed to do was daydream about Jack and doodle his name in the margin of her yellow notepad. The telephone rang, snapping her out of her reverie.

"Hi, Tess." The sound of Jack's deep voice caressed her through the receiver. She smiled in spite of herself, knowing she'd never tire of hearing him say her name.

"How are you feeling?" she asked, winding the cord around her index finger as she spoke.

"Better, although I still feel like an idiot for showing up on your doorstep drunk last night and then falling asleep. I don't drink very often. Not like that anyway. As for this morning, I won't apologize for that." He waited a heartbeat before adding in a low voice that made Tess melt, "I haven't stopped wanting you."

"Well, I've done some thinking about that," she admitted, grateful he couldn't see her furious blush. "I...I want you, too."

Jack thought his heart would explode. Her reply surprised him. He had expected another conversation where he verbally stalked her and she retreated, content to let their physical attraction smolder. The thought had occurred to him as he'd stood under a frigid shower spray earlier in the day that perhaps Tess's reluctance had less to do with not wanting to engage in sex than never having experienced it. She was passionate when pushed, but she also exhibited a maidenly sense of modesty that seemed quaint by today's standards.

"Tess, are you sure?" he stammered, feeling the need to give her an out. His conscience nudged him. He'd been putting a lot of pressure on her, perhaps too much. The fact that she had finally given in made him uneasy suddenly.

"I'm sure," she said softly.

"Why?" he asked, his voice cracking. He cleared his throat and tried again. "I mean, what made you change your mind?"

She hesitated, and Jack wondered if she planned to reply at all. Finally, she said, "We're both adults, Jack. I think the reason I changed my mind should be obvious."

"I suppose," he said hesitantly.

"W-want to come over tonight?"

They were the bold words of a sexually liberated woman, but to Jack, Tess sounded more like an uncertain virgin offering herself up for sacrifice. He blew out a ragged breath and shook his head, unable to believe what he was about to say.

"I want to, Tess. You have *no* idea how much I want to. But I think we'd better sit tonight out, give ourselves time to think straight about this."

"You said earlier that we think too much," she reminded him unnecessarily.

"Yeah, I know, but this is a big decision. We

shouldn't enter into it casually. It could complicate things between us.''

"Jack, have you changed your mind?"

"Not on your life!" he exclaimed. With a snort, he added, "I just seem to have developed a conscience where you're concerned." It helped, he amended silently, that she wasn't within arm's reach, otherwise, he knew his noble intentions would have been discarded along with their clothing.

"I'm a fully grown woman. I believe I can make up my own mind when it comes to having sex," Tess replied, sounding more than a little insulted. "I want to have sex. With you."

Hearing her put it so bluntly made his blood hum, but he took a deep breath and forged ahead. "Believe me, Tess, I know you're a woman, but I also know...that is, I get the impression..." He stumbled around for the right words, before blurting out: "Tess, are you a virgin?"

"Yes, I'm a virgin," she confirmed, sounding hurt and a little defensive. "Jeez, Jack, you say it like I've got some kind of disease. So, I've never been with a man before. It doesn't mean I'm incapable of having sex or making the decision to have sex."

"I didn't say you were."

"So, do you want to have sex with me or not?" she yelled impatiently into the phone.

The invitation had never been put to Jack quite like that, and the absurdity of their argument wasn't lost on him. Their second fight, it seemed, was over sex. Even more ludicrous, it was as if they had stepped into some parallel universe: *she* wanted sex, and *he* was arguing with her to wait. He rubbed his eyes with an index finger and thumb, and let out a weary breath.

"I want to have sex with you. That's not the issue here. I just don't want to give you the wrong impression." His tone softened. "I don't want you to think I've changed my mind about where this is heading."

"Here we go again," she sighed. "I *know* you don't want a serious relationship. You've made that abundantly clear, Jack. Everyone may think we're engaged, but I *know* the truth. I *know* that we've never so much as gone out on a real date together."

"I—I didn't realize," he said, feeling like a selfish jerk. He'd pawed at her, hounded her, thrown her life into chaos, caused friction between her and her family, imposed on her for a dozen favors, and made her tell twice as many lies. Yet, he'd never even taken her to dinner, unless it was to further his cause. He opened his mouth to apologize again, but she cut him off.

"You've *told* me that you don't plan ever to marry anyone. You've *told* me that you won't marry me, no matter what everyone else in Pleasant River thinks. If this is about my ordering the dress—"

"No, Tess," he interrupted. "It's not about the dress. I just don't want to take advantage of someone who has been nothing but kind to me. Can you understand that?"

"But you won't be taking advantage of me," she insisted.

"Okay, okay," he said, forestalling further argument. "But take some pity on me tonight, please. I'm just too tired to do my best work." Then, all teasing humor gone from his voice, he added quietly, "I want it to be special for you."

She all but broke his heart when she replied, "If it's with you, Jack, it will be special."

"Well, now that we've settled that," he said, his voice oddly husky, "It should be clear it doesn't have to happen tonight. There's no need to rush."

"Okay," she agreed. She sounded equally relieved and disappointed that he would not be coming over.

"So, what time should I pick you up tomorrow morning?" he inquired, now that the subject of sex appeared to be safely behind them.

"Quarter to nine is fine. The church is only around the block from me. Um, are you Catholic, Jack?"

"A fallen-away one, but yes." He tried to remember the last time he had risen early on a Sunday morning to attend church services. He'd been a boy, he realized, and his parents had still been married to each other. A lifetime ago.

"Good," Tess sighed. "I'm sure my mother has been worried that we wouldn't be getting married in the Catholic Church, even though she's been too polite to ask." She cleared her throat a little self-consciously. "As for the dress, I'm sorry I didn't mention it before Betsy did. I just felt so foolish that I got talked into ordering it."

"It's all right. I know how that goes. I've got Davis standing up for me now," he said with a humorless chuckle. "If we're not careful, Tess, we'll be making up guest lists and picking out dinner menus before long."

"So, what do you think about beef tips and grilled salmon?" Rita asked. The family was seated around her small kitchen table eating broccoli and cheese quiche, and sipping orange juice. Tess noticed that an extra place was set at the head of the table for a mysterious "special" guest who had yet to arrive.

"I talked to Emma Baker yesterday at the beauty shop and she said they had Sue Ellen's reception at the Saint Sebastian last summer, and that's what they served. It's really not that expensive to have your reception there," she said, sending Tess an encouraging little smile. "I have some money set aside for retirement that I could take out."

"Absolutely not!" she shouted, regretting the outburst when her mother's expression turned from one of excitement to one of embarrassment. While she thought of some way to more gracefully decline her mother's kind offer, Jack spoke up.

"That's very generous of you, Mrs. Donovan, but what Tess means is that I have some money I inherited from my grandmother. We had planned to pay for the wedding ourselves. I hope that doesn't offend you?"

"No, of course not," she said, her smile only a little awkward. "I always wanted Tess to have a beautiful wedding like the one her father and I threw for Betsy. It's a relief to know that she'll have it. A girl only gets married once."

A girl only gets married once, Jack repeated to himself. He thought about disputing that, but he realized that to people like the Donovans, such a statement was indeed true. They married once, for love, and honored those quaint vows that his parents seemed to keep repeating again and again without ever managing to make them stick. He looked at Tess. Innocent, kind, smart, loyal, loving. She would be a beautiful bride, a wonderful wife. But not his. He vowed to himself then and there that he wouldn't compromise her. The least he could do was leave her with her virginity and self-respect so that when she finally met the right man she wouldn't regret having given herself to Jack first.

"Don't worry about Tess, Mrs. Donovan. Her happiness is very important to me."

Rita laid a small, work-calloused hand over his. "Jack, don't you think it's about time you started calling me Mom?"

He stared back, dumbstruck. Over the years, there had been many women who could have qualified for that title. A virtual parade of them had filed in and out of Jack's life, staying only long enough to ensure a divorce settlement from his weak-willed father. But Rita sat across from him offering something so totally alien to him that he didn't know quite how to respond. An uncomfortable silence stretched around them.

"Well, you don't have to," Rita said, snatching her hand back to fuss with her napkin. "I just thought since that's what Brian calls me..."

"No, it's not that. I don't even call my own mother Mom," he admitted in a quiet voice. "Tess knows about my family."

His mouth worked, but he couldn't seem to continue. He was overwhelmed to be surrounded by people who would embrace him so completely in so brief a period of time. He'd never known such unconditional acceptance. It humbled him, and it made him want things he had long ago told himself weren't for him: a wife, love, family ties.

Tess's heart lurched when Jack turned to her, his expression so full of baffled anguish that she started to reach out to him. She wanted to ease the pain she saw reflected in his eyes, but her fingers had barely grazed the cuff of his sleeve when he rose abruptly from his chair and bolted from the room.

"Oh, dear!" Rita exclaimed. She looked at Tess, who was wiping away tears from her eyes. "I feel just horrible. I never meant to make him uncomfortable or to bring up bad memories."

"Mom, it's not your fault," Tess assured her. "I doubt Jack even realized how he felt about his family life until you asked him to call you Mom. His father's been married five times," she explained. "And he's rarely seen his mother in all the years since his parents divorced."

"Oh, I had no idea," Rita said.

"I think I'll go after him."

Tess slipped from her chair and went in search of Jack. She found him just outside the back door, sitting on the edge of her mother's leaf-covered porch. He wasn't wearing a coat, but he didn't seem to notice the dipping temperature or the bone-chilling wind.

Rubbing her hands briskly over her arms, Tess sat down beside him. "Are you okay?"

He gave her a sheepish little smile that didn't reach his eyes before turning back to stare out at the small, fenced yard.

"She asked me to call her Mom. Do you know that when I was fourteen, my own mother asked me to call her Janice? Apparently having a teenage boy around calling her Mother was cramping her style. She was between husbands and dating a man to whom she had lied about her age, so the woman who gave birth to me went from being Mother to being Janice."

"I'm so sorry, Jack." Tess wrapped her arms around him in a fierce hug, wishing she could absorb some of his misery.

"Your mother has known me all of a few weeks. She has every reason *not* to like me. She didn't know about our engagement, which isn't really an engagement anyway. She calls your apartment yesterday morning, and I'm there after having spent the night, but she has the class not to throw that in my face today." He expelled a disgusted sigh. "I've done my level best to seduce her daughter, and the lady not only wants to dip into her retirement funds to throw us a big, splashy wedding reception with all the trimmings, she asks me to call her Mom." He shook his head in genuine wonder. "You're really lucky, Tess."

"I know. I take my family for granted sometimes, but I know." She gave him a final squeeze, then kissed his cold cheek. "Come on, let's go back inside where it's warm. Even if it's only for a little while, Jack, I'd like to share my Mom with you."

"Thank you." He leaned over and kissed her lips, not with the searing passion of the day before, when he had reduced her to a puddle of incoherent hormones. This kiss was uncalculated and infinitely sweet. And, Tess knew it was the most intimate moment they had ever shared.

Hands linked, they walked back into the house, where Jack was spared making awkward explanations—a new guest had joined the family around the table, and they were all chatting amiably.

"Father Riley," Tess wheezed. "This is a surprise." She glanced at her mother, who smiled brightly.

"I hope you two don't mind," Rita said. "I invited Father Riley to brunch so we could talk about the wedding."

"It's a good thing your mother talked to me last week or you might have had to postpone your wedding until July," said the portly priest who had presided over all of her family's major functions, from baptisms to her father's funeral. "I have only one Saturday free in June."

Jack caught Tess's panicked look and gave her shoulders a gentle squeeze. "Aren't we lucky, honey? July would be out of the question." He added lying to a priest to his already lengthy list of sins.

Even a scoundrel had to draw the line somewhere, and Jack drew it at allowing Tess to lie to a man of the cloth. So for the next forty-five minutes, while Tess sat in a dazed stupor, Jack answered the priest's questions and officially set the wheels for their make-believe nuptials into motion. Before they managed to make their excuses and leave, they had signed up for marriage classes, settled on a ceremony time, and tapped Brian to walk Tess down the aisle.

Chapter Eight

Tess spent the following week dodging phone calls from her mother and sister. When she couldn't get out of talking to them, she kept the conversations brief, offering the excuse that she was too busy studying for final exams to think about wedding plans. There was a ring of truth to her evasions, but deep down she knew that eventually she would have to face them. And, she knew, eventually she and Jack would have to stage their breakup.

Tess dreaded that day. She knew that once the entire town believed they had broken up, it would be difficult, if not impossible to keep seeing one another. As it was, she hadn't seen him since Sunday. He had started his new job and was in the midst of moving into his new home. But whenever Tess suggested coming over in the evenings, whether to help him unpack or to bring take-out, he found a reason to say no. If it hadn't been for their nightly phone conversations she might have worried that he wasn't interested in her any longer.

Tess had just finished washing her face and was rubbing moisturizer over her cheeks when the phone rang. The smile that had her lips curving was involuntary, the fluttering in her stomach wholly female. Jack always called at ten o'clock.

"Hi, handsome," she said.

"Hi yourself, gorgeous. So, how did your poli-sci quiz go?" he asked. He sounded truly interested. That was one of the reasons Tess looked forward to these nightly conversations. Beyond the flirtation that made her heart palpitate and her body burn, they also spoke of dreams and ambitions, grand plans and simple observations. He seemed to care about the things that were important to her.

"I think I aced it. Hey, guess what." She didn't wait for him to reply, rushing ahead with, "Mr. Applebee called this afternoon. I have an official interview with him and the publisher next week. I think it's all just a formality. I mean, they know my work ethic and capabilities, but I plan to wear a suit and bring a portfolio of my clips anyway. If I get the job, I'll start full-time at the end of January when the other reporter leaves, even though I won't be quite finished with school."

"That's great!"

She basked in his enthusiasm, but felt the need to point out, "It's not the *New York Times* or even the *Detroit News*."

"But it's important to you," he said and she got the feeling he truly understood how much this one small, long-held dream of working at her hometown paper mattered to her.

So she shared another one with him. "I want to be the first female editor of the *Beacon* some day." The words came out in a rush, spoken just above a whisper. This was a secret ambition she had confided in no one—until now.

"And you will be," he said simply, making her smile bloom.

They exchanged small talk and pleasantries for the next several minutes, and then Jack said, "You mentioned the other day that we've never so much as gone out on a real date. I'd like to remedy that situation. Saturday good for you?"

"Hmm." She pretended to think about it. "I might be able to clear my schedule."

"I'll pick you up around noon. Wear something casual and plan to spend the whole day with me."

Jack arrived on her doorstep just as snowflakes began to sift through a cloudy sky.

"It's freezing out here!" Tess cried, grateful for the thick wool sweater and turtleneck she wore beneath her coat. He reached the car ahead of her, and, as always, insisted on opening her door. Inside, the car was warm and cozy. Christmas carols played on the stereo.

"Christmas is my favorite time of year," she commented as Jack drove. She hummed along to "Jingle Bells." Then Bing Crosby began to sing "White Christmas," and Tess sighed. "I absolutely adore Bing. No one sings Christmas carols quite like him."

"I'm glad to hear you like Christmas, because I thought we'd drive over to Piedmont to do some shopping, buy some ornaments since I don't have any, or haven't found them yet in all the boxes, and then pick up a tree on the way home.'' He slanted her a look. ''If you play your cards right, I'll throw in dinner.''

''No date can be considered official if you don't feed me,'' she teasingly informed him.

''Well, then, I will. If I'm not mistaken we pass a burger joint or two along the way.''

That comment earned him a playful punch in the arm.

Forty minutes later, they reached their destination. It seemed to be the destination for the entire state. The mall's parking lot was nearly filled to capacity. Jack gave up trying to find a close space and parked the car what seemed like five city blocks from the mall's entrance. He had offered to drop Tess at the door and meet her inside since it had begun to snow in earnest, but she declined.

''I don't think a little snow will hurt me,'' she told him. But after the first blast of wind made her eyes water and her cheeks sting, she grabbed his hand and ran through the parking lot, dodging cars and slushy puddles in her hurry to get inside.

''Come on, before we freeze to death!'' she hollered. She chuckled when he skidded briefly on an icy patch, nearly sending the pair of them sprawling on the asphalt.

They reached the entrance, breathless and laughing, and stood just inside the door stamping their feet and shaking off the snow. When Tess saw Jack's expression grow serious, a different kind of breathlessness stole over her.

Jack's laughter faded as he watched Tess. She looked so beautiful, her porcelain skin glowing with health, snow glittering in her hair. He reached over to brush the flakes away, his fingers twining through red silk. Fire and ice, he thought, as contradicting as the innocently passionate woman before him.

He lowered his head and kissed her, intending the contact to be quick and playful. But, as often happened around Tess, his plans changed. While harried shoppers bustled in and out of the doors around them, the kiss deepened until he gave serious consideration to returning to the car. Shopping and his honorable intentions be damned.

"Hey, get a room!" a male voice boomed. They jolted apart, the reality of what they had been doing and where crashing over Jack in a violent wave of embarrassment. One look at Tess told him she felt the same way. Her face had turned a festive Christmas red.

"Davis, Marianne," Jack said, trying to sound nonchalant. "What a surprise. Tess and I thought we'd do some shopping."

"Did you find anything in her tonsils?" Davis asked dryly.

Jack accepted his friend's razzing. He had little doubt that Davis and Marianne were quite surprised by the passionate and very public scene they had just witnessed. Jack didn't go for such displays of affection. Handholding, fine. Maybe a quick hug. But he'd all but had Tess on the floor. He couldn't explain it to himself. He wouldn't even try to explain to anyone else.

"Thought I spotted some mistletoe," he improvised.

Marianne, bless her heart, changed the subject. "Did you guys just get here?"

"Yeah. After we finish shopping, I thought we'd pick up a tree on the way home," Jack said.

"A real tree?" Davis's eyebrows shot up. "This from the man who had that white plastic monstrosity in his living room last year? What happened, Nancy take the tree when she left?"

Tess's forehead wrinkled in confusion, and she looked from Davis to Jack. "Who's Nancy?"

"Now you've done it," Marianne muttered. "Come on, you big dolt." She grabbed her husband by the arm and hauled him away as he sputtered apologies and goodbyes.

"Who's Nancy?" Tess repeated, standing her ground as a tidal wave of shoppers streamed around them.

"An ex-girlfriend," he said simply, hoping that would be the end of it. The mutinous expression on Tess's face told him otherwise. So he added impassively, "She and I lived together."

Tess's heart squeezed painfully as she contemplated his revelation. He didn't owe her any explanations, but for some reason it hurt to know that while he had refused to offer her any long-term relationship, he had set up housekeeping with someone else. She schooled her expression into one she hoped reflected only polite interest and asked, "Oh, for how long?"

"A few years."

"What happened?" she asked, then held up a hand. "No, no let me guess. That pesky commitment thing came up, right? After a few years, I'd imagine she wanted to make your relationship more permanent than being roomies."

He nodded slowly. "Something like that."

"When did it end?"

"Seven months ago. She moved out."

Seven months, Tess thought dejectedly. Surely, he couldn't be over someone who had so recently shared his life, his home, and his bed.

"Did you love her?" The words came out on a shaky breath before it occurred to Tess that she had no right to ask him such a personal question. She had no rights at all when it came to Jack Maris. She might love him, she might want to make love with him, but he didn't owe her any explanations. She was on the verge of telling him to disregard her question when he answered, his tone as frosted as the mall's big windows.

"I don't see how that matters at this point. She's engaged to someone else. It's over."

Jack regretted his curtness instantly, but it shamed him to realize that he had not loved Nancy the way he should have loved the woman who shared his home. The proof was that he didn't miss her. He didn't know what it said about him that he could live with someone for three years, date her exclusively for six, and yet a handful of months after it ended barely recall how she looked or even how she had felt naked and warm in his arms.

And now he'd hurt Tess. He could see that in her stricken expression. Whether they were really engaged or not, it didn't matter. She deserved to know that the man she claimed to want in her bed had so recently come from someone else's.

"You still in a mood to shop?" he asked. "I'll take you home if you don't want to spend the day with me."

Jack had taken off his gloves, and Tess watched him slap them against his thigh. The gesture should have seemed impatient, but it struck her as nervous instead. And she noticed that his expression had turned from foreboding to contrite.

"I still want to shop." She pasted a bright smile on her face, and though her heart felt as if it were splintering into a million tiny, jagged pieces, she pointed to the bookstore. "Let's start there. My sister loves a good mystery."

They wandered through the first several stores in silence. Then the beautiful decorations that hung throughout the mall and the Christmas carols that floated just above the din of shoppers started to work their magic. She and Jack exchanged a few tentative smiles. Finally he had her laughing in earnest when he donned a Santa's hat and asked if she wanted to sit on his lap.

"You're incorrigible," she sighed.

"And you're beautiful, especially when you smile." He swiped the red hat off his head and held it in his hands. Staring at it, he asked, "Are you mad at me? For not telling you, I mean."

She shook her head. "It just caught me off guard, is all. It's not like I thought you hadn't ever dated someone before. I just didn't realize you had so recently come away from such a serious relationship."

"Serious," he repeated, his tone oddly self-mocking.

"Well, it's none of my business, anyway," she said, hoping to dismiss the painful subject once and for all.

He caught her hand. "Tess, don't do that."

"Don't do what?"

"Act as though you don't matter to me. I think we've established that what we have goes beyond you doing me a favor. We may be only pretending to be engaged, but I'm not pretending when I say you're special to me. I have feelings for you.''

"I have feelings for you, too.''

The words were a pale imitation of the love she felt, but they would have to do, since his feelings came with limitations and qualifications, and hers were proving to be heartbreakingly boundless.

Tess had put a major dent in her Christmas shopping list, to say nothing of her bank account, when Jack said, "Let's take a breather and get something to drink. I'm parched."

It was nothing short of a miracle that they found an empty table in the mall's crowded food court. While Tess guarded their mound of shopping bags, Jack went in search of beverages. He returned fifteen minutes later carrying two lemonades and a couple of soft pretzels.

"This doesn't qualify as dinner, does it?" She arched an eyebrow.

"No. I just figured we could use some fortification before we head out among the masses again."

They sipped their drinks and nibbled the pretzels in companionable silence. From their vantage point they could see the mall's replica of Santa's North Pole home. They watched as parents struggled to keep their antsy children entertained in the long line to visit with Saint Nick. Toward the back, a tyke of about four managed to escape his mother's tired grasp. He bulleted away, running full out, determination stamped on his pixie face.

Jack laughed as he and Tess watched the exasperated mother's frantic efforts to snag the boy as he weaved in and out of the line with all the finesse of a receiver going for a touchdown. He reminded Tess of the errant tot who'd first "introduced" her to Jack with the help of a bowl of chili. She smiled at the memory. Fate, her mother would call it. And maybe it was.

"Looks like he's going to make it," Jack commented, sounding pleased.

The boy was almost to the front of the line, but before he could burst onto the stage where Santa sat on an ornate throne with a squalling toddler perched on one knee, a woman dressed as an elf reached out and hauled the boy back.

They watched the mother take her son from the elf and march him away. Clearly, he would not be seeing Santa this day. He seemed to realize it too, and sent up an ear-splitting wail.

"Uh-oh. He's not happy now," Jack said. Then he surprised her by asking, "You ever wonder what kind of parent you'll be?"

"Sometimes. I think I'll be patient. My mom's real patient," Tess explained. "What about you? What kind of parent do you think you'll be?"

"I don't know. I doubt I'll ever be a parent," he said. Then he frowned, as if he just realized how much that bothered him. "I don't have the best role models, not like you've had."

"That doesn't mean you'll be a bad parent, Jack. My dad bounced around in foster care until he was twelve. Then an older couple adopted him. They were kind in their own way, but very strict. But my dad was a most loving father." She smiled warmly, remembering his booming laughter and velvet discipline.

"I wish I could have known him," he said. "I would have liked to meet the man who helped raise such a giving, gifted daughter."

His compliment warmed her. "I wish you could have, too."

Jack shook his head. "Something tells me he wouldn't be all that happy with me as a prospective son-in-law."

"No, he'd like you," Tess insisted. "He'd respect your business sense, the way you set a goal for yourself and go after it. You wanted the VP job at Faust and you got it. You can be very single-minded."

"Sometimes *single-minded* is just another word for ruthless. I got the job at Faust because I lied. Ira Faust wanted to hire a family man. I made sure that's what he thinks I am. Or will be." He took a sip of his drink and shook his head. "Doesn't say much about me, does it?"

"Hey, don't talk about my fiancé that way," she said, trying to lighten the mood. "I'll tell anyone who asks that you're pretty terrific. Kind, smart, funny, good-looking. A great kisser." She sent him a winsome smile, before adding softly, "Don't be so hard on yourself, Jack."

"Yeah, but what are you going to say about me after everyone thinks I've called off the wedding? People will expect you to be angry or hurt."

"Still playing me for the dumpee, are you?" She rolled her eyes in mock exasperation. "I've decided I want to do the dumping. I'll try to let you down gently, but I can't make any promises."

"Tess, I'm being serious. We have to decide how best to handle things. I think the more public the better." He seemed to contemplate the matter for a moment before adding, "Maybe I'll come by the diner, and we'll have a scene there."

She didn't want to think about breaking up, not now. She put up a hand to silence him.

"There are two weeks left before Christmas. I don't want to talk about this between now and then." She issued the request in a quiet, sober voice. It was too hard to talk about endings when her heart wanted to concentrate on beginnings.

"Okay," he agreed reluctantly. "We're only post-poning the inevitable, but we don't have to talk about it right now."

He finished his drink and set the empty paper cup on the table. "Ready for more shopping?"

The sun was dipping low in the sky and more than three inches of snow blanketed the car when they finished buying out the stores.

"So, where to now?" she asked as Jack maneuvered the car out of the mall's parking lot.

"I thought we'd go eat. There's a steak place up the road a few miles. Davis told me about it a while back. He said the food's good and the atmosphere is casual. Then I thought we'd stop at the nursery that's just off the interstate. You know, the one near the Pleasant River exit. They've got a pretty decent selection of trees on the lot."

Jack flipped on the radio, then pushed in a Christmas CD. As Nat King Cole sang about chestnuts roasting over a fire, Jack reached over to take Tess's hand. It seemed right somehow, necessary even, to touch her. He was still holding it when they reached the restaurant.

* * *

Tess was determined to enjoy her first real date with Jack. Granted, it had gotten off to a rocky start, what with talk of ex-live-in girlfriends and their own impending breakup, but it finally seemed to be back on track.

"What looks good to you?" Jack asked from behind his menu.

They were seated in a high-backed booth that gave them some privacy. Jack had been right about the casual atmosphere. Even wearing blue jeans, Tess didn't feel out of place. But the restaurant had charm, from the chuck wagon that doubled as a salad bar to the bucolic paintings that adorned the walls. It wasn't as fancy as the Saint Sebastian, but she liked it. She smiled across the table at Jack, enjoying herself immensely.

"I'm thinking I'll have the surf and turf. It's the most expensive thing on the menu. I'm making up for lost time," she teased.

The waiter ambled over just then, wearing a gray cowboy hat and black leather vest.

"Are you ready to order?" he asked politely.

"Yes. I'll have the New York strip, medium well. The lady will have the surf and turf, cooked the same. Baked potatoes okay with you?" he asked Tess. She nodded, fighting back a grin. She hadn't really wanted the surf and turf, but now she was stuck with it.

"And I'll have a tossed salad, French dressing. Tess?"

"Oh, I'll take Italian on mine, please."

"Very good," the waiter said. "And to drink?"

"I'll take a beer."

"The same," Tess said.

As the waiter left with their orders, Jack said, "A

beer drinker, huh? I had you pegged for wine, or some trendy drink.''

''Nah,'' she waved a hand. ''Wine gives me a headache. As for mixed drinks, you never know quite how strong they'll be. But a bottle of beer is a bottle of beer. Not much anyone can do to it, so I always know my limit.''

''Are you always so logical?''

''I used to think so,'' she admitted. ''When it comes to things like school and work and family obligations, I'm incredibly logical. I figure out what needs to be done and when, then I find a way to do it.'' She tilted her head to the side. ''But you're different. I'm not logical at all when it comes to you.''

Jack was flummoxed. Tess said it so simply, no game-playing, no guessing. He'd never met another woman like her. She was special, all right. And too good for the likes of him.

''Involving you in this mess may have been a mistake. But it's the best mistake I ever made. I'll never regret it, Tess,'' he said, his voice hoarse with emotion. She looked away quickly and blinked a few times, and Jack realized his words had sounded a little too much like a goodbye.

''I'll never regret it either,'' she whispered.

But Jack had a sick feeling that she would.

''I like the Scotch pine,'' Tess said, leaning forward to smell the evergreen's fragrant boughs.

Jack shook his head and indicated the seven-foot Douglas fir on the other side of the aisle. ''I'm thinking this one.''

''Well, it's your tree,'' she said with a shrug. ''If you don't want to take my advice...''

Jack rolled his eyes and pulled a coin from his pocket. "Heads I take home the fir," he announced before flipping the quarter into the air with his thumb.

Ten minutes later they were trying to secure more than six feet of Scotch pine onto the roof of his sports car. As Tess helped, she was thankful Jack had had the foresight to bring some rope. As it was, on the short drive home, she kept expecting the tree to fall off.

At his house, Tess held open the door while Jack stumbled inside, his face obscured by the prickly branches. He set it up in the living room, moving aside a recliner to position it in front of the bay window. The scent of pine filled the room as she watched him struggle with a string of lights, and she opened boxes of newly-purchased ornaments.

"How is it these things can be tangled when I just bought them today?" Jack asked. He was sitting cross-legged on the floor amid a jumble of cords and colored lights. Tess decided to take pity on him and offered a hand. Together, they strung the lights on the tree, then hung the ornaments. When they finished, Jack flipped the light switch and they stood back to admire their handiwork.

Tucked securely against his side, Tess said, "We make a good team."

"Yes, we do."

It felt as if her heart had stopped beating when he turned to look at her, his luminous green eyes rich with promise. He traced a fingertip down the curve of her cheek.

"Jack," she whispered on a sigh and closed her eyes.

The kiss began gently, a slow exploration that

made her shiver with anticipation. She gripped his broad shoulders, holding on as it gained momentum and edged toward greedy. Big hands circled her waist, pulling Tess flush against him. She heard him moan, a low rumble that issued from the back of his throat, before she felt his fingers skim up her spine beneath the thick sweater and turtleneck she wore. They stopped at the clasp of her bra, fumbled there for a moment, then abruptly—unbelievably—they stilled. His breathing short and labored, Jack leaned his forehead against hers, smoothed down her sweater, and set her away from him.

"Tess, it's…" He cleared his throat and looked away briefly before continuing. "It's getting pretty late."

Jack had to summon up every ounce of his willpower to say the words. Even so, he tucked his hands into his trouser pockets just to be on the safe side. He didn't trust them not to reach out, to touch and take. He considered himself a man of principle, but with five feet nine inches of gorgeous redhead within arm's length, he was sorely tempted to break his vow to leave Tess a virgin.

It was one thing to flirt with her and kiss her in public. That was safe. But with a bedroom just down the hallway, and her looking up at him with those smoky, sexy eyes, it took the will of a saint to say, "I think I'd better take you home. I've got to be up early."

"I see," she replied with a proud tilt of her chin, but she was unable to keep the hurt from seeping into her voice when she added, "I'll just get my things."

"Tess." He wanted to explain, but she had turned away and was slipping into the shoes she'd taken off at the front door. He stopped her as she reached into the foyer closet for her coat.

"Tess, I like you too much to start something that I know you'll want to continue. And it won't be able to continue, because you won't be satisfied with the kind of relationship I can offer you."

"Why are you so sure you're incapable of making a commitment to me?" she demanded, swiping angrily at the tears that spilled over her lower lids, and taking a dirty streak of mascara with them. She looked irate and miserable, and he called himself a dozen kinds of fool for hurting her.

"I love you, Jack," she said. "Sometimes, I think that maybe, if you gave it a chance, you might love me back. Why can't you even try?"

That declaration had him taking a wobbly step backward. She couldn't possibly, his head insisted, so his tone was a little more gruff than he intended when he said, "You don't love me, Tess. You think you do, but it's lust, hormones, nothing more."

From the look on her face he knew he had just hurt her even more.

"Don't tell me what I feel!" she shouted. She struggled into her coat while Jack watched, too befuddled by her words to be a gentleman and help. "It might be hormones for you, Jack Maris, but don't diminish what I feel for you by saying it's mere lust. I may never have felt like this before, but I know what it is. I love you."

In a flash she was out the door, calling over her shoulder, "But don't worry, I'll get over it."

"Tess!" he hollered, as she disappeared into the night. "Oh for pity's sake," he grumbled as he stepped into his shoes and yanked his coat off the hanger. He banged out the door in a panic, skidding and sliding on the slippery walk as he struggled into his coat. He walked up the street several houses in one direction, and then several houses in the opposite direction, but he didn't find her. *Where could the woman have gone so quickly?* he wondered, as the first tentacles of fear slipped around his heart and squeezed. Surely, she couldn't be angry enough to try to walk home. It was nearly five miles, the sidewalks were icy, and the hour was closing in on eleven. Pleasant River was no murder capital, but crime could happen anywhere. He hurried to his car. He would drive around town in search of her, he decided. If he didn't find her he would call her sister and alert the police, then wait on her doorstep until she finally put in an appearance.

As it turned out, his plan became moot. Tess sat in the passenger seat of his car, arms folded across her chest, lips compressed into a thin, stubborn line.

"I guess I'll take you home now," Jack remarked dryly as he slid onto the driver's seat. Relief quickly turned to irritation when she continued to stare out the window in stony silence.

"You're acting childishly, you know." He turned the key in the ignition and backed down the drive, continuing his lecture. "I'm right about this, Tess. And some day you're going to be grateful that I didn't let things progress any further between us." He turned to look at her in the dim interior of the auto-mobile, just barely able to make out the mutinous tilt of her chin. "I want you. But I don't want you to hate me, and you would."

"Why do you suddenly insist on making my de-cisions for me?" she asked wearily. "What would have happened if I had given in the first time you made a pass? Or if Brian and Betsy had shown up a little later that morning in my apartment?''

"We'd both hate me," he said quietly.

They drove in silence down his street, past the festive lights and colorfully decorated homes that earlier had seemed so cheerful. Bing Crosby's "Joy to the World" played on the CD player, his silky voice caressing each note, but Jack noticed Tess didn't hum along this time.

He was almost to her street when he decided to try one last time to make her see the soundness of his decision.

"Tess, please don't be mad. I'm doing what I think is right. For both of us. If we make love, you'd want more than just a casual relationship. You'd want the whole package."

"If you mean I'd want you to be faithful and committed, yes, that's the package I'd want." Arms crossed tightly over her chest, she continued to stare out her window.

"No, you'd want more. Eventually, you'd want much more than I could give you. And you'd deserve it, Tess. You shouldn't settle for less."

She turned to look at him, her heart shining in her eyes. "Neither should you," she said, climbing out of the car before he could even park, much less open her door.

The next few days passed in a weary haze. Between working at the diner, taking final exams, and preparing for her interview at the *Beacon,* Tess managed not to think too much about her relationship with Jack. Or the fact that it seemed to be ending. But the night before her meeting with Mr. Applebee, she couldn't sleep. With the clock's hour hand closing in on midnight, she lay awake in her bed, thinking about nothing else.

Jack had called. Several times now, in fact. But she'd let the answering machine take her messages. It was cowardly, she knew, but she didn't want to rehash old ground or move on to plotting their public breakup. Not just yet, she told herself, a tear slipping down her cheek. As she wiped it away, the telephone began to ring. From down the hall she heard her voice invite the caller to leave a message after the beep, then Jack's voice, just a tad frustrated, came through loud and clear.

"Come on, Tess, pick up. *Please.* I know you're there." Silence hummed for a moment, then, "I want to wish you good luck tomorrow on your interview. I know you'll do fine. They'll hire you." More silence. "Tess?"

She lay in her bed, holding her breath. She wanted to pick up the receiver on the extension, but she didn't. "Good night," she whispered when she heard him say the same.

Chapter Nine

"**I** got the job?" Tess repeated, feeling so dazed that she worried she had merely imagined the offer of full-time employment with two weeks of paid vacation and health benefits.

Mr. Applebee and the *Beacon* publisher, Mr. Devon, sat across the conference table. It was the editor's begrudging expression, more so than Mr. Devon's grinning nod, that told her she had indeed been hired as a full-time reporter. She would cover education to start—city hall being too plum a beat for a rookie to hope for right off the bat, but she didn't care. By the end of January, she would be drawing a decent paycheck for her efforts, and, just as important to Tess, *Staff Reporter* would appear below her name on the byline rather than the generic *Contributing Writer*.

Tess thanked them profusely and gathered up her portfolio. She was still grinning like a fool when she bustled through the *Beacon*'s revolving front door and ran headlong into Jack.

"Someone's on cloud nine," he said, reaching out a hand to steady her. In his other hand he held a bouquet of pink carnations. "So, how'd it go? Or do I need to ask?"

She stared at the flowers, her heart lurching around in her chest. He'd been waiting for her, she realized, waiting with flowers to offer his congratulations or condolences, whichever the case may be. But even knowing why he'd come, she asked, "What are you doing here?"

He shrugged and looked away briefly as he tucked a hand into the pocket of his overcoat. "You wouldn't take my phone calls."

"I've been busy."

His gaze slid back to hers, and it said he didn't believe her excuse. His voice lowered a notch when he asked, "Do you hate me Tess?"

I love you! She wanted to shout the words, but even then she knew that Jack wouldn't hear them. Not really. He didn't understand them because he didn't love her back. More hurtful, he didn't think she *could* love him. Lust, he'd called it. The memory ripped through her heart like jagged glass.

"I have to go," she replied, stepping around him and ignoring the bouquet he held out for her. "I've got one more final to study for before my shift at Earl's."

"Tess, wait!"

But she hurried to her car, driving away without ever looking back.

The diner was crowded, thanks to another of Earl's advertised specials. Tess blew out an exhausted breath and pulled the order pad from her pocket. A nasty headache pulsed behind her eyes, and she felt like something that had been scraped off the bottom of a shoe. Despite securing the newspaper job she'd dreamed about for years and having given Earl her two weeks' notice, her mood was anything but celebratory, and the reason was seated in what had been the diner's only available booth.

She pasted a bland smile on her lips and brought Jack a menu along with a glass of ice water, deciding to treat him with polite indifference.

"Place is hopping," he said, taking a glance around. "I thought you would get off at six tonight."

"Annabelle called in sick. I told Earl I'd stay late."

"You're working too hard," he commented, reaching out to touch her arm.

His kindness would be her undoing, she thought, so she steeled herself and, all brisk efficiency, she said, "You could make my job easier if you gave me your order. The fish is on special, all you can eat with fries for $6.95. Soup of the day is chili. Oh, and we're all out of the pork chops. You have to come early if you want Earl's famous pork chops."

He nodded uncertainly. "I'll have a grilled chicken sandwich. So, did you get the job?"

"Yes." She watched his proud grin unfold, but steeled her heart. "Anything to drink?"

"Coffee. That's great, about the job. I figured as much." She waited for him to mention the flowers that she had all but tossed back in his face, but he only said, "When do you think you'll be off? I thought we could talk."

"I'm really tired, Jack."

Jack felt like a heel. Her weariness showed. The bulky winter coat she'd worn that afternoon had hidden the fact that in just a week she seemed to have lost weight. Her sleek curves now appeared a tad more angular beneath the pink uniform. And here he was pressing her, but he needed this resolved. He had to make her understand once and for all why he wouldn't make love to her, and why she couldn't really love someone like him.

"I could drive you home, or meet you there. We need to settle some things."

"Miss!" A diner at the next table waved a hand to get Tess's attention. And from the kitchen, Jack heard a gruff voice holler, "Order up!"

"Excuse me." She left without giving him an answer.

For the next fifteen minutes, he watched her flit around the restaurant, refilling coffee mugs, balancing trays laden with plates of food, wiping down tables as the occupants left them. She looked as if she would fall over, but somehow she managed to stay upright, turning in meal orders and handing out checks with a brittle little smile quirking up the corners of her mouth.

"Sorry your dinner took so long," she apologized, setting the plate in front of him. "We're a little busy tonight."

"I see that." Then he reminded her, "You never answered my question."

A couple of diners had lined up at the cash register, waiting for her to ring up their bills. She sent them a hurried smile, and called, "I'll be right there."

Before she could scoot away again, however, he snagged her hand. "Tess?"

"Jack, I don't have time for this right now."

"That's my point. So, after work?"

Why did he have to do this here of all places, and now, when she could hardly think straight? Tess looked around at the crowd of diners. Several of them were trying to get her attention, raising empty coffee mugs or even waving their hands. The pair at the register were frowning and looking at their watches.

"Oh, to heck with it," she said, her voice rising just enough that conversations quieted around them. Jack's brow puckered in surprise at her irritated tone. "You said you wanted it to be public, right?" she hissed quietly between gritted teeth. She didn't give him a chance to respond. "I'm sick of it, Jack!" she screeched. "Sick of the lies, sick of trying to make myself believe this is going to work. I thought my loving you could be enough, but it's not."

The tears that filled her eyes were real.

"The wedding is off!" she yelled on a sob, as the diners stared at them in slack-jawed shock. Even Earl had come out of the kitchen to gape at the spectacle occurring in his dining room. No doubt all of the juicy little details would be swirling around town before the eleven o'clock news aired. In a town this small, their very public breakup just might *make* the eleven o'clock news, she thought.

And that was before the chili.

Tess didn't know where the idea came from, whether it was her flair for drama or the hurt churning in her stomach that made her snatch up Mattie Henderson's half-eaten bowl of Earl's five-alarm concoction. But whatever lay behind the impulse, she carried it through.

"I believe this is where it all started," Tess said.

Smiling sweetly, she up-ended the bowl, dumping the tepid contents into his lap, crackers and all.

Another suit ruined, she thought, pushing the beginnings of remorse to the corner of her conscience. She would not feel guilty, she told herself. He had wanted their breakup to be believable, after all.

She stormed away in a swish of pink cotton. She didn't stop to offer any apologies to Earl, whose mouth worked soundlessly as she stomped past. She pushed open the swinging doors to the kitchen and walked through them with the dangerous swagger of a gunslinger, slowing down only long enough to grab her purse and coat out of the small room off the kitchen. Then she yanked opened the back door that exited into the alley.

Anger carried her all the way to her car, but then it deserted her, leaving only heartbreak. She didn't drive home. She was too devastated to sit alone in her apartment and mourn what might have been. She drove to Betsy's instead, arriving on her sister's doorstep with a tear-stained face, sobbing so uncontrollably that Brian wanted to whisk her off to the hospital emergency room, sure she had been assaulted.

"N-n-no," she sniffled. "I'm f-fine."

She sat on the couch in their living room. Betsy sat beside her, simultaneously offering words of comfort and pressing tissues into her hand, as Brian paced the room, looking decidedly oversized and helpless in the presence of a woman's tears.

"Tell us what happened, baby," Betsy coaxed, reverting to the well-remembered role of big sister.

"J-J-Jack and I..." Tess tried to get the words out, but they bunched in her throat and were lost to another bout of weeping.

"Aw, honey, did you and Jack have a fight?" Betsy asked. She stoked the hair back from Tess's damp face. "It must have been some fight. Is it about the wedding?"

"There isn't g-going to be a w-wedding."

"Of course there is. You say that now, but after you two talk it out, you and Jack will make up and put this disagreement behind you."

"N-no," Tess shook her head miserably. "You don't understand. W-we were never really engaged. It w-was all a lie. Oh, God, but I fell in love with him anyway. And now it's o-over. I dumped chili in his l-lap."

She saw Betsy and Brian exchange baffled glances before she covered her face with her hands and sobbed even harder.

"Maybe you'd better start at the beginning," Betsy said.

"You look like heck."

Davis leaned against the open door of Jack's office at Faust Enterprises, feeling utterly unsympathetic as he watched his best friend engage in what appeared to be a life-and-death struggle with an aspirin bottle. The bottle was winning.

"Stupid child-proof caps," Jack muttered darkly. "No one can open the things."

Davis sauntered into the room and held out a hand, deciding it best to step in before his friend got the bright idea of using the pointy letter opener sitting on the desk blotter.

"Allow me." Davis took the bottle and asked, "How's the head feel?"

"Like someone is using my temples for bongo

drums. Tension headaches,'' he muttered, carefully lowering his head into a pair of shaky hands. "My life didn't have tension until I took your advice."

Davis took his friend's surly tone in stride. After opening the bottle with a simple flick of his thumb, he shook out two white tablets. "Here, take these, maybe they'll improve your mood."

"I doubt that," Jack said. He tossed the pills into his mouth and chased them down with a shot of black coffee. "So, what are you doing here anyway, besides making my life miserable?"

Davis held up a hand, fending off the insult. "And it's nice to see you, too, pal. Actually, this isn't quite a social call. I just came by to drop something off." When Jack continued to hold his head and moan, Davis added, "If it's any consolation, Tess looks worse."

Jack's head snapped up at that. He winced, but asked, "Tess? When did you see Tess?"

"About ten minutes ago. She came into my office wearing dark sunglasses." Davis cocked his head to the side, feigning ignorance. "Odd, wouldn't you say, since it's cloudy outside? I asked her what was going on, but she was feeling about as chatty as you are this morning."

Jack hadn't thought it possible, but he felt even worse. He remembered how Tess had looked the night before, tears glittering in her smoky eyes, and he had known then that her words were not part of some script, but spoken from her heart. The heart he had broken.

"What did she say?" he asked Davis, hope rising like a phoenix from the ashes of the past twelve hours of misery.

"Nothing, really." Davis dug into his front trouser pocket and extracted something. "But she did ask me to give you this." He set the diamond ring on the desk blotter, then sank into the chair across from Jack. "Care to tell me what happened?"

"It's over."

"What's over? The sham engagement?"

"Yeah. That, and everything else."

"Jack, you're crazy about her. Don't deny it. Why end it all? Why not keep—"

"Keep dating?" Jack interrupted. He blew out an impatient breath. "Come on, Davis, how would that look? Everybody in this town thinks we're getting married. Now they know we're not. If we keep seeing each other, people might get the wrong idea."

Davis shook his head, irritation surging well ahead of pity in his tone when he replied, "Do you even hear yourself? You're throwing away the chance of a lifetime because you're worried about what people will think."

"That's not it, not really." Jack sighed with weary resignation. "It's best this way."

"Best for who?"

Jack glared at his friend. "Do you think this is easy for me? It's not. Tess is special. Really special," he stressed. "She doesn't deserve to be hurt."

"Yeah, well if you're so worried about hurting Tess, you're too late, pal. From the way she looked this morning, I'd say she's long past hurt and well on her way to devastated." Davis leaned forward in his chair, his tone one of challenge as he continued, "When it comes to getting hurt, I don't think Tess is the one you're worried about."

"Just what are you saying?" Jack fired back. If

they hadn't been such good friends he might have bolted around the desk to take a swing at his friend. He couldn't remember ever being this angry with Davis.

"I'm saying, *you're* afraid of getting hurt." Davis said boldly, although Jack did notice the man's Adam's apple skitter nervously up and down his throat. "I'm saying that you love Tess, and it's scaring you. I'm saying you're being a coward."

When he'd finished his revelation, he sat back in his chair seeming to wait for the fireworks to begin. Jack decided not to disappoint him.

"You don't know what you're talking about," he bit out angrily. He got up and paced the room, throwing out explanations and rationalizations as he wore a path in front of the window. "I'm not cut out for the long-term, and you know it. Things would go bad, really bad, then they would end. Tess would wind up hating me." He laughed a little harshly. "Right after she scalped me in a divorce settlement."

"Oh, so you've thought about marriage, have you?" Davis crossed his legs and slouched back in the chair. For some reason, the relaxed pose made Jack even more irritated. It was as if his friend knew something he didn't, and it made Jack nervous.

"It was pretty hard not to think about marriage when her family had us picking out china patterns." He shot Davis a disconcerted look, and grudgingly conceded, "You were my best man, by the way."

Davis nodded solemnly. "I wouldn't have expected it to be otherwise. But that's wedding stuff, Jack, I asked if you'd thought about marriage. They're two distinctly different animals, you know. One is short-lived and idyllic. The other is long-term and all stark reality.''

''That's precisely my point,'' Jack said. He walked back to the desk and stared at his Grandmother Maris's diamond engagement ring. ''I'm not cut out for long-term.''

''Yeah, so you keep saying. But I notice you never disputed my assertion that you love Tess.''

''I don't.... It's not that....'' He blew out a frustrated breath and sank into his chair. ''It doesn't matter.''

Davis snorted. ''That's the first really stupid thing you've said. And believe me, you've been offering up some real tripe ever since I walked in here. Let me ask you something, did you love Nancy?''

''Davis, I don't see the relevance.''

''Just answer the question. Did you love her? You spent six years with her,'' he prompted helpfully.

''I thought I loved her, but...'' Jack shrugged, embarrassed. ''I don't know now.''

''What changed your mind? Or should I ask who?''

''Okay, I see your point. You're saying that until I met Tess I didn't know quite what I'd been missing. You're saying that Tess showed me what a pale imitation of love I had been contenting myself with, and that maybe that's why it didn't work out with Nancy. Maybe I could have a long-term relationship with Tess because I never felt for Nancy in more than six years what I feel for Tess in less than six weeks.''

Davis blinked. ''Well, that wasn't quite what I was saying, but it works for me. Did you just hear yourself?''

''What if it doesn't work? What if we invest several years of our lives in a relationship and then break apart as bitterly as my parents did, making a couple of kids into casualties in the process?'' He picked up the ring and turned it over and over in his agitated fingers, wishing it had some magical power to bestow happiness on whatever union it symbolized.

"But what if it does work? Why don't you ask yourself that?'' Davis walked around the desk and placed a hand on Jack's tense shoulders. "Marianne and I have had plenty of disagreements and fights. We've hurt each other, but we always make up. When you want something badly enough, Jack, you *make* it work. You sacrifice your pride, you learn to bend when necessary, and you *make* it work. So the question, Jack, is how badly do you want this to work?''

Tess sat in her car in the parking lot and cursed her bad luck.

"As if I don't have enough problems,'' she muttered while the old car's motor whined and sputtered but refused to catch. She thumped the steering wheel with the palm of her hand and wished she had a cell phone.

Well, there was no help for it. She was going to have to call a cab, which meant going back into the building and possibly running into Jack. Mumbling a mild oath, she pulled on her dark glasses and returned inside. The lobby receptionist knew Tess by name, and like the rest of Pleasant River, she'd already heard about the breakup. She offered Tess the same gratingly sympathetic smile she'd given her half an hour earlier when Tess had asked to see Davis Marx, but thankfully the woman asked no questions while she placed the call.

"You can wait over there," the receptionist said when she hung up, motioning to a small sitting area.

Tess had barely taken her seat when she spied Jack. He emerged from a hallway near the reception desk carrying a stack of papers. He was talking to another suit-clad man, so he didn't see her. Still, she pressed back in her seat, hoping to be obscured by a potted palm tree. From behind green fronds, she tipped down her dark glasses and studied him. There was little comfort in the fact that he looked almost as bad as she did. His eyes were shadowed and hollow, his cheeks in need of a shave. Even his gorgeous hair looked mussed, as if he had ravaged it with frustrated fingers.

"Tess, your cab's here!" the receptionist called to her helpfully, although Tess noticed she looked in Jack's direction as she spoke. Tess wanted to strangle her, but that would take too much time. Instead, she hopped up and bolted for the door, dignity forgotten in her rush to avoid another torturous confrontation.

"Wait!" she heard Jack holler, but she didn't so much as break stride. She shoved her way through the exit, yanked open the cab's door and jumped inside.

"Drive!" she ordered, panting from exertion and a surge of adrenaline.

As the taxi sped away she dared to look back. Jack stood at the curb, his head thrown back and his eyes clenched shut. *He looks almost heartbroken,* she thought. Then, *No. I must be mistaken. Jack might be sorry about hurting me, but ultimately, he's relieved it's over.*

Jack returned to his office, his heart throbbing worse than his head. He slumped into his chair, recalling Davis's words. But it wouldn't matter how badly he wanted things to work if Tess couldn't stand the sight of him. And clearly, she couldn't.

"Can I have a moment of your time?" Ira Faust asked politely from the doorway, interrupting Jack's thoughts.

"Of course," he said, hoping the discussion would not be about his broken engagement. Hope died quickly.

"I heard that Tess called off the wedding," Ira began once he had settled into a chair. Jack might have been amused by Ira's interference, or even appalled that an employer would butt into his private life, but he felt too raw to summon mirth or outrage over the idiosyncrasies of small-town living.

"Yes, last night." When the older man just stared at him, Jack went on. "We've been having some problems, a disagreement." Deciding it best to keep the explanation vague and semi-honest, he finished, "It just didn't work out, sir."

"Nonsense," Ira declared emphatically, his jowls quivering. "You surprise me. You're giving up too easily. My Cora begged off at least five times before I managed to drag her to the altar. Women can be temperamental, my boy. You've got to cajole them. You've got to woo them, and," he tapped an arthritic finger to his temple, smiling slyly, "you've got to make them think it's all their idea."

"Well, in this case, I think Tess would just as soon murder me as be cajoled."

Ira chuckled almost fondly. "I heard she dumped a bowl of Earl's chili in your lap."

"Yeah." Jack chuckled, too, albeit self-consciously. Then he remembered the way she had looked at the time, all fire and shattered pride, wielding a bowl of chili like some angry goddess ready to strike him down with a lightning bolt. "She's got great aim," he commented half to himself. "And one heck of a temper. I'm just grateful Earl keeps the really sharp implements in the kitchen."

"Nothing quite like a feisty woman." Ira leaned forward and confided, "Cora once threatened me with a frying pan for tracking mud on the kitchen floor. 'Course I was three sheets to the wind at the time, four hours late coming home, and I'd forgotten it was our fifth anniversary."

Jack winced. "How'd you get out of it?"

"I did the manly thing." Ira winked. "I groveled."

"I don't think Tess is interested in seeing me grovel. I don't think she's interested in seeing me, period."

"Well, I'd imagine a real relationship is harder to work out than a phony engagement." His dry tone accompanied a bland expression. He'd be one heck of a poker player, Jack decided.

"You knew?"

"I'm old, my boy, not senile," Ira replied dryly. "I had suspicions from the first." He leaned forward and added, "Tess never seemed the sort to keep something that important from her family. I didn't know for sure, though, until today."

"Today?" Jack's stomach did a queasy little roll.

"There's a very riled construction worker in the lobby who claims you broke his sister-in-law's heart, and very possibly compromised her virtue. And while he'd like to throttle you himself, I think he'll settle for having you dismissed."

Jack closed his eyes and shook his head, feeling

resigned. The position that had meant so much to him mere weeks ago didn't seem important now. Nothing did.

"I'll have my things cleared out by the end of the day. Just for the record, sir, I didn't set out to deceive you. It's just that you seemed to want a family man, and, well, I didn't have any immediate prospects in that area. I want to apologize for lying to you. And for involving Tess in this. But, sir, I didn't…that is, I never compromised Tess Donovan."

He stood up, intending to start cleaning out his desk, but Ira motioned for him to sit.

"You're not going anywhere, and your apology is accepted. I'm sorry I may have compelled you to lie. You're very perceptive." He rubbed his balding head and sighed. "I did want to hire someone with a family. I know such a qualification could get me sued today, but Faust Enterprises started as a family business. I wanted that tradition to continue with my successor."

"It's a fine tradition, sir. I just don't know if I'll be the one to carry it on. I hadn't thought I'd ever marry. And now, well, I've made a mess of things with Tess. If you want to reconsider your offer, I'll understand."

"No," Ira said confidently. "I don't want to reconsider. I have complete faith in you."

That simple declaration pleased Jack inordinately. Perhaps at thirty-two he should have been beyond needing positive reinforcement, but after the day he'd had, his waning confidence appreciated the boost.

Ira scratched his head. "But may I ask, how exactly did you meet Tess? You had just arrived in town, after all."

The memory had Jack grinning. "I ate at Earl's after our initial interview. She dumped chili on my lap that time, too."

"Ah, the ruined suit," Ira replied, apparently recalling that Jack had arrived at the second interview wearing khakis.

"Yeah, one of a matched set now as it turns out."

Ira chuckled as he rose. "Well, young man, it's Christmas Eve, and the wife wants me home early." His smile was paternal when he added, "Why don't you leave early, too? Go set things straight with your girl."

Jack frowned. "Unfortunately, she's not my girl."

"Not yet, maybe, but I imagine my vice president is capable enough to overcome that obstacle." Ira winked slyly. He was almost out the door when he turned and held up a finger. "By the way, Brian Hopper is still in the lobby."

Chapter Ten

Jack could see Brian pacing impatiently in front of the receptionist's desk. He wore his quilted brown work coat over a pair of stained coveralls of the same color. He looked huge and positively livid, and that was before he spotted Jack.

"You!" He pointed a thick finger in Jack's direction. "I want to have a word with you."

"I'll bet more than one," Jack muttered under his breath as he led Brian to the same sitting area where Tess had waited for her cab.

The minute they stopped walking, Brian poked a finger in Jack's chest and demanded, "Who do you think you are? Playing with Tess's emotions, playing with her entire family's emotions. The Donovans are fine people. The best. And I won't stand by and watch them messed with by some pretty-boy hotshot from Boston!"

Although the pretty-boy comment grated, Jack accepted the tongue-lashing as his due. He even tolerated the finger that lanced his breastbone, but he felt the need to point out, "I never made Tess any promises. I used incredibly poor judgment spinning the lie I did. I'll apologize to you and the entire family for that. The Donovans are a wonderful family, as you said, but Tess knew from the beginning that the whole thing was a lie. She knew we weren't really engaged."

Brian's lip curled in contempt. "Sure, she knew. But that didn't stop her from falling in love with you. She showed up on our doorstep last night sobbing hysterically. Knowing didn't stop her from getting hurt." Punctuating each word with a thrust of his index finger, he enunciated, "And I blame you for that."

Jack turned and paced a couple of steps away. He resisted the urge to rub his sore chest, instead he ran a shaky hand through his hair. He remembered exactly how Tess had looked the night before when she had delivered her farewell diatribe—and the bowl of chili. Brian was right. It didn't matter that she'd known there wouldn't be a wedding. Jack had managed to hurt her anyway. And the guilt gnawing his gut told him that the fact he'd hurt her unintentionally didn't make her pain any less potent.

"She okay?" he asked in a quiet voice.

"What do you care? You got what you wanted."

His back still to Brian, Jack only nodded.

The righteous anger that had spurred Brian to drive to Faust Enterprises and inform Ira Faust of Jack's duplicity seemed to ebb a little, leaving uncertainty in its wake, as Brian asked, "You did get what you wanted, didn't you?"

Jack had never figured he'd experience the greatest

epiphany of his life on Christmas Eve while facing the wrath of an irate construction worker, but as he stared at the faded striped wallpaper in the company's reception area, he finally had an answer to his own doubts and to Brian's simple question.

"No, I didn't."

Brian shuffled his feet, misunderstanding. "I didn't mean to get you fired. I just, oh heck, I was angry and shot off my mouth to Faust without thinking. I guess I'll apologize to you for that."

Jack turned around then, shaking his head. "No need to apologize. I still have my job. What I don't have is Tess."

Brian opened his mouth, then shut it again, before he finally said, "I'm sorry, I'm having a hard time following this conversation."

"I love Tess." So simple, Jack thought, once he'd finally said the words he'd spent a lifetime eschewing and avoiding. Meaningless words, he'd told himself, because he'd never had the emotions to back them up. Now he knew their potency, and while it should have scared the heck out of him, he could only marvel at their power and pray they would be enough to win back the woman who had inspired them.

"I love Tess," he repeated, smiling this time.

Brian ran a hand across the back of his neck, clearly baffled by this latest revelation. But then he seemed to relax, as if accepting Jack's sincerity.

"Yeah, well it's a good thing, or I was going to have to kick the living daylights out of you!" he said, his voice gruff with emotion. He slapped Jack hard on the back instead. "I know someone who'll be happy to hear this. Come by the house tonight. Tess will be there. Rita, too."

Jack had hoped for something more private, but this might be better, he decided. If he stopped by her apartment, she probably wouldn't let him in. At least at her sister's house he would have a way in the front door. And, he reasoned, he owed her entire family an apology for the hurt he had caused.

"What time?"

"We're having dinner at six. Rum-spiked eggnog and Mom's famous angel-food cake afterward. Of course, you'll be having humble pie," Brian put in. A ghost of a grin had his lips twitching.

Ah, yes, Jack thought, perversely enjoying the fact that Tess's brother-in-law would never let him live this one down.

"I'll be there. But don't tell Tess I'm coming. The way she feels about me right now, I wouldn't put it past her to bolt the door and call the cops."

Brian nodded his agreement. He had zipped up his jacket and was tugging a black knit cap onto his head, when a thought occurred to him. With almost comical outrage, he sputtered, "You spent the night in her apartment!"

"Yeah, well, you dropped me off," Jack pointed out. Now that balance seemed somewhat restored between the two men, he relaxed. He shoved his hands into his front trouser pockets and smiled devilishly as Brian's eyes narrowed in good-humored accusation.

"I felt sorry for you! I thought you were engaged."

"You didn't feel sorry for me," Jack disputed, enjoying the lighthearted debate, enjoying the under layer of friendship that made it possible. "You wanted me to suffer. You knew I wanted Tess. And you knew I was too drunk to do anything about it that night."

"And the other nights?" The laughter ebbed into something else. Something protective and challenging. Something Jack respected and admired.

"I never touched Tess," Jack said quietly, his gaze steady and sincere as he looked at Brian.

Brian nodded once, then humor leaked into his sober expression. "You poor slob," he muttered, without a trace of sympathy. "See you tonight."

"Merry Christmas!" Brian held open the door while Tess bustled inside, her head barely visible above the mound of brightly wrapped presents loaded in her arms. When he took the packages from her, he noticed she looked tired and subdued, but she hardly resembled the overwrought female who had pounded on their door the night before.

"Hello, Brian," she said, trying on a smile that failed to reach her eyes. He wished he could tell her then and there that Jack loved her, but true to his word, he kept his mouth shut. As added insurance, he hadn't told his wife or mother-in-law, either. He knew them. The word *secret* had a different meaning in their vocabulary.

Betsy rushed forward to take Tess's coat. As Tess slipped off her boots, Rita swooped in from the kitchen, bringing with her the scents of corned beef and cabbage. It was a Donovan family tradition to have corned beef and cabbage on Christmas Eve. She wiped her hands on the flowered apron she wore and came forward to envelop her youngest daughter in a mother's soothing embrace.

"How are you doing, sweetie? Betsy told me about Jack." She shook her head. "I don't understand why you lied, but I'm sorry it didn't work out." She held

Tess at arm's length and clucked her tongue. "You look so pale."

"I'm okay, Mom, promise. I'm just so sorry about lying to you." Tess's eyes pooled and her voice grew thick as she babbled her apology and explanation. "It seemed harmless enough at first, then it just snowballed. I didn't want to lie to you, and then I fell in love with him, only he doesn't feel the same way. Now, everything's a mess."

Rita shook her head. "No, Tess, I can't believe that all Jack's feelings were manufactured. Some things are meant to be."

"Fate, Mom?" Tess asked on a watery laugh.

Rita smiled. "Fate, destiny. Surely, once Jack's had time to think clearly about this, he'll realize he loves you, too."

Tess shook her head in dejected disagreement. Brian wanted to tell them the truth, but with an effort he held his tongue as Rita said, "Come into the kitchen, and help me with dinner while your sister sets the dining-room table."

Nerves jangling, Jack slowly pushed open the kitchen door. This was the most important meeting of his life, he just hoped he wouldn't blow it. Tess stood at the sink, her slender back to him. Her mother was seated at the table, preparing a salad. Rita's cheery chatter dried up when she spied Jack.

She sent him an encouraging little smile and said, "Tess, dear, there's someone here to see you."

When Tess turned around and spotted Jack, he heard her suck in a surprised breath. She wore a festive poinsettia-print apron over a sober black skirt and sweater, and her hair was plaited into a conservative braid. Except for the apron, she looked like a woman in mourning, and Jack longed to comfort her.

"Tess," he whispered, and watched her expression momentarily soften. Then her gaze turned remote. He fisted his hands at his sides to keep from reaching out to her.

Rita looked from one to the other as the tension built. She sent Tess a quiet smile and then apparently decided to leave them alone to work out their differences. At the door, she paused and in a voice low enough to reach Jack's ears only, she whispered, "Take care not to hurt her anymore, young man. She's strong, but even steel can bend under the right circumstances."

He nodded, never looking away from Tess.

"I won't, Mrs. Donovan. I promise I'm done hurting your daughter."

As Rita started past Jack, she surprised him by whispering, "I told you to call me Mom."

His head whipped around, and he blinked, a little uncertain that he had heard her right. But she smiled knowingly, and he could only grin in return. His smile evaporated when he looked back at Tess. She was staring at him, her expression cold and unapproachable.

It took Tess a moment to steady herself enough to speak. She couldn't believe he was here, standing in Betsy's small kitchen, looking so devastatingly handsome in his sports coat and pleated trousers.

"I'm surprised to see you here." She wrung out a soapy dishcloth and turned to tackle the food-spattered countertop with a vengeance. Over her shoulder, she added, "I thought we discussed everything last night."

"No." He stepped forward until he stood just behind her. "You dumped chili in my lap and basically told me to get lost. But I didn't get a chance to rebut anything you said, so I don't believe that constitutes a discussion."

She turned and found herself nearly nose to nose with him. She bowed back over the countertop and took a calming breath. *I can do this,* she told herself. *Even without a room full of spectators, I can give the performance of my life.*

"Jack, it had to end. You've told me that from the beginning. So I ended it, and very publicly, so that the entire town is aware that our June wedding is very definitely off. What more is there to talk about?"

Jack heard the reasonable tone, and it gave him pause, but only for an instant. She couldn't look at him when she said the words. A woman who meant goodbye would look a man in the eye, he told himself. So he concentrated on remembering the way she had felt in his arms, wild with passion and promise. And how, just days ago, she had professed to love him. Surely, she could not have changed her mind so quickly, no matter how much cause he might have given her. He gripped the ring in his hand a little tighter, feeling the diamond bite into the flesh of his palm. The pain was as real as the commitment he wanted to make.

"Well," he began. "There's the fact that you love me. How about we start with that?"

She sucked a quiet breath between her teeth and shimmied past him, as if eager to put some distance between them. Betsy's kitchen, however, was small, so she had to settle for putting the brief expanse of a Formica-topped table between them.

"Love's funny, Jack. When only one person feels it, well, it wears out pretty fast," she informed him coolly. "I'll get over you in no time. There's really no need to worry about my feelings."

Strange, Jack thought, but he doubted the hole in his heart would ever heal completely if he lost Tess.

"Really?" he said, edging around the table. "Tell me more. I seem to find myself in need of knowing exactly how that works."

Her chin shot up. "You're not being very kind," she said with quiet dignity.

"No, I'm not being kind," he agreed, his gaze solemn as he took another couple of steps forward. She backed up until the wall prevented further retreat. "What I am is a man who's just realized what an idiot he's been. What I am, Tess Donovan, is a man who has finally figured out that he's fallen in love."

When she only shook her head, eyes filling with tears of disbelief and desolation, he tried again. "I love you, Tess. Only you. And you love me, too. At least you did. And I think you can again." He was rambling, words rushing out in idiotic sentences. None of this was going as he'd planned. Jack barreled ahead anyway. He had no pride now. "Besides, you miss me. I know you do. I...I have it in writing."

He fished his wallet out of his trouser pocket and pulled her letter from the billfold. Hand shaking, he held it out to her. "See. It's all here in black and white. Signed even."

"You kept this?" she whispered, tugging the letter from his hand. He watched her eyes swim with tears and she choked on a sob that splintered his heart in two. He couldn't stand it any longer. He pulled her into his arms, where she shuddered against him, each ragged breath a lash to his heart.

"I love you," he repeated fiercely, hugging her tightly. "I know I took the scenic route getting here, but please don't tell me I'm too late. Please don't tell me that, Tess."

"Scenic route's fine," she said finally, gazing up at him through tear-misted eyes. "But next time, Jack Maris, just remember to take me along for the ride."

"Aw, Tess," he sighed, as his lips dipped to hers. This kiss was unlike any other they had shared. He infused it with tenderness and contrition, and she answered with forgiveness. When it ended, he maneuvered her into a kitchen chair.

"I have something for you," he said.

"I have something for you, too. I left it in my car. I was going to drop it off on your doorstep on my way home tonight. Why don't we go into the living room with the others and open our gifts? Maybe Mom will let us break with tradition and open them before dinner," she said with endearing eagerness.

He shook his head. "That's not what I meant."

Slowly, his gaze never wavering, he got down on one knee before her, and Tess would later swear to their children that for one brief moment her heart simply stopped beating.

"Tessa Claire Donovan," he began, taking her hand as he knelt in front of her. "You are the *only* woman I will ever love. I may not come from a family that knows how to keep the commitments they make, but I promise you that I love you enough to do everything possible to make this work. I want to grow old with you. I want to make children with you. I want to wake up every morning and see you there beside me in our bed. Will you do me the honor of becoming my wife?''

The smile that bloomed on her face gave him a glimpse of the radiant bride she would be.

''Oh, Jack,'' she whispered, and leaned forward to cup his face between her hands. ''Yes,'' she said, kissing him softly on the lips. ''Yes, I'll marry you.''

''Thank God,'' Jack sighed.

Her voice strong and steady, Tess said, ''I love you.''

''I won't get tired of hearing that every day for the next fifty years or so.''

''Nor will I,'' she promised.

* * * * *

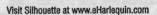

If you enjoyed what you just read,
then we've got an offer you can't resist!

Take 2 bestselling love stories FREE!

Plus get a FREE surprise gift!

You're not going to believe this offer!

In October and November 2000, buy any two Harlequin or Silhouette books and save $10.00 off future purchases, or buy any three and save $20.00 off future purchases!

Just fill out this form and attach 2 proofs of purchase (cash register receipts) from October and November 2000 books and Harlequin will send you a coupon booklet worth a total savings of $10.00 off future purchases of Harlequin and Silhouette books in 2001. Send us 3 proofs of purchase and we will send you a coupon booklet worth a total savings of $20.00 off future purchases.

Saving money has never been this easy.

I accept your offer! Please send me a coupon booklet:

Name: _____

Address: _____ City: _____

State/Prov.: _____ Zip/Postal Code: _____

Optional Survey!

In a typical month, how many Harlequin or Silhouette books would you buy <u>new</u> at retail stores?

☐ Less than 1 ☐ 1 ☐ 2 ☐ 3 to 4 ☐ 5+

Which of the following statements best describes how you <u>buy</u> Harlequin or Silhouette books? Choose one answer only that **best** describes you.

☐ I am a regular buyer and reader
☐ I am a regular reader but buy only occasionally
☐ I only buy and read for specific times of the year, e.g. vacations
☐ I subscribe through Reader Service but also buy at retail stores
☐ I mainly borrow and buy only occasionally
☐ I am an occasional buyer and reader

Which of the following statements best describes how you <u>choose</u> the Harlequin and Silhouette series books you buy <u>new</u> at retail stores? By "series," we mean books within a particular line, such as *Harlequin PRESENTS* or *Silhouette SPECIAL EDITION.* Choose one answer only that **best** describes you.

☐ I only buy books from my favorite series
☐ I generally buy books from my favorite series but also buy books from other series on occasion
☐ I buy some books from my favorite series but also buy from many other series regularly
☐ I buy all types of books depending on my mood and what I find interesting and have no favorite series

Please send this form, along with your cash register receipts as proofs of purchase, to:
In the U.S.: Harlequin Books, P.O. Box 9057, Buffalo, NY 14269
In Canada: Harlequin Books, P.O. Box 622, Fort Erie, Ontario L2A 5X3
(Allow 4-6 weeks for delivery) Offer expires December 31, 2000.

PHQ4002

where love comes alive—online...

your romantic
life

> Talk to Dr. Romance, find a romantic recipe, or send a virtual hint to the love of your life. You'll find great articles and advice on romantic issues that are close to your heart.

your romantic
books

> Visit our *Author's Alcove* and try your hand in the Writing Round Robin—contribute a chapter to an online book in the making.

> Enter the *Reading Room* for an interactive novel—help determine the fate of a story being created now by one of your favorite authors.

> Drop into *Shop eHarlequin* to buy the latest releases—read an excerpt, write a review and find this month's Silhouette top sellers.

your romantic
escapes

> Escape into romantic movies at *Reel Love*, learn what the stars have in store for you with *Lovescopes*, treat yourself to our *Indulgences Guides* and get away to the latest romantic hot spots in *Romantic Travel*.

All this and more available at
www.eHarlequin.com
on Women.com Networks

Desire celebrates Silhouette's 20th anniversary in grand style!

Don't miss:

• *The Dakota Man* by Joan Hohl
Another unforgettable MAN OF THE MONTH
On sale October 2000

• *Marriage Prey* by Annette Broadrick
Her special anniversary title!
On sale November 2000

• *Slow Fever* by Cait London
Part of her new miniseries FREEDOM VALLEY
On sale December 2000

Plus:

FORTUNE'S CHILDREN: THE GROOMS

On sale August through December 2000
Exciting new titles from Leanne Banks, Kathryn Jensen,
Shawna Delacorte, Caroline Cross and Peggy Moreland

Every woman wants to be loved...
BODY & SOUL

Desire's highly sensuous new promotion features stories
from Jennifer Greene, Anne Marie Winston
and Dixie Browning!

Available at your favorite retail outlet.

Silhouette ®

Where love comes alive™

Visit Silhouette at www.eHarlequin.com

PS20SD

COMING NEXT MONTH

#1480 HER HONOR-BOUND LAWMAN—Karen Rose Smith
Storkville, USA

He was tall, dark and older, and he took her in when she'd had no home…or identity. When Emma Douglas's memory returned, she believed she and Sheriff Tucker Malone could have a future. But would the honor-bound lawman she'd come to love accept her in his bed…and in his heart?

#1481 RAFFLING RYAN—Kasey Michaels
The Chandlers Request…

"Sold for $2,000!" With those words wealthy Ryan Chandler reluctantly became earthy Janna Monroe's "date" for a day. Though bachelors for auction seemed ludicrous to Ryan, even crazier was his sudden desire to ditch singlehood for this single mom!

#1482 THE MILLIONAIRE'S WAITRESS WIFE—Carolyn Zane
The Brubaker Brides

For heiress turned waitress Elizabeth Derovencourt, money equaled misery. But her family, not their fortune, mattered. So she visited her ailing grandmother…with a dirt-poor denim-clad cowboy in tow as her "husband." Only she hadn't banked on Dakota Brubaker's irresistible charm—or his millions!

#1483 THE DOCTOR'S MEDICINE WOMAN—Donna Clayton
Single Doctor Dads

Dr. Travis Westcott wanted to adopt twin Native American boys, which was why he welcomed medicine woman Diana Chapman into his home. But somehow the once-burned beauty made Travis want to propose *another* addition to his family: a wife!

#1484 THE THIRD KISS—Leanna Wilson

The first kiss was purely attraction. Brooke Watson and Matt Cutter didn't believe in lasting love. But everyone else did, particularly their nagging families, which was why Brooke agreed to playact the tycoon's beaming bride-to-be. Yet as a *real* wedding date loomed, was a happily-ever-after possible?

#1485 THE WEDDING LULLABY—Melissa McClone

Their marriage had lasted only one night. No problems, no heartache. But unexpectedly Laurel Worthington found herself expecting! When she told father-to-be Brett Matthews her news, he insisted they marry ⸱⸱ᵃin. But Laurel wasn't about to settle for anything but the *real* ⸱⸱ n ring….